# Writing How-To Articles & Books

## Share your know-how and get published

GW00496592

## Studymates Academic Books

Algebra
Better English
Better French
Better French 2
Better German
Better Spanish
Better Welsh
British History 1870–1918
Chemistry: chemistry calculations explained
Chemistry: As chemistry explained
European History
Genetics
Hitler and Nazi Germany 3rd Ed
Lenin, Stalin and Communist Russia
Organic Chemistry
Plant Physiology
Poetry
Practical Drama
The Theatre Makers
Shakespeare
Social Anthropology
Statistics for social sciences
Study skills
The Academic Essay
The English Reformation
The War Poets
Warfare

## Studymates Writers Guides

Kate Walker's 12 Point Guide to Writing Romance
Starting to Write
The Business of Writing
Writing Crime Fiction
Writing Historical Fiction
Writing How-to Articles and Books
Writing Travel
Writing TV Scripts

## Studymates Post-Graduate Guides

Your Masters Thesis
Your PhD Thesis

## Studymates Professional

Growing Workplace Champions
Project Management

# Studymates
### Helping You to Achieve

# Writing How-To Articles & Books

## Share your know-how and get published

## Chriss McCallum

www.studymates.co.uk

ISBN: 978-1-84285-095-4

First published in 2008 by Studymates Limited.
PO Box 225, Abergele, LL18 9AY, United Kingdom.

Website: http://www.studymates.co.uk

Typeset by Vikatan Publishing Solutions, Chennai, India
Printed and bound in Europe

# Contents

Contents

## 7 **Writing the article**                               **91**

## 8 **Writing a how-to book**                             **111**

# List of illustrations

# Author's note

All books, magazines and publishing companies mentioned in the text are valid and current as I write. However, I can't offer you any guarantees that they will all still be around by the time you read this book, publishing in the twenty-first century being every bit as volatile and unpredictable as it has been since humans progressed beyond chiselling hieroglyphs in stone.

Be a smart writer—check out every market for yourself.

# Foreword

I am inspired. I am only one chapter into Chriss McCallum's book and already there are a dozen ideas buzzing around my brain which were not there before. Or I did not recognise them as ideas.

I've done the self-assessment exercises at the end of the same chapter and learned a great deal about myself. There were many things which I had forgotten about or pushed to the back of my mind. Revelations, ambitions, disappointments. My life in a nutshell. And it is all material for reader-related writing.

In her book, Chriss has generously given us access to her secret weapons, told us about her forensic eye and the editorial calendar. She knows that the market out there for how-to material is huge, with magazines devouring good tips, fillers and articles every week and every month. Walk around the magazine shelves at W H Smith's and you're looking at a mountain of work. Business magazines are particularly lucrative, we're told.

But Chriss also tells us what not to do. How the scatter-gun approach is every editor's nightmare. She stresses the importance of market research and how to do it, so that our work doesn't go to an inappropriate market and waste everybody's time and temper. Also the necessity of keeping good records, both for yourself and for the tax man.

There are also excellent tips on book signings, interviews and being interviewed, and if we get lucky, appearing on television.

It's all written in clear, clean English that we can understand and appreciate. No redundant words. I can't wait to get started.

*—Stella Whitelaw*
*How to Write Short-Short Stories*
*How to Write & Sell a Proposal*
*How to Write & Sell a Synopsis*

# Introduction to 'how-to' writing

'How-to' is the key to one of today's biggest markets for articles and books. This market exists because people are looking for help.

There is an ever-growing demand for instruction and advice on how to make things, how to do things, how to achieve goals, live better, make money, save money, feel good, look good...

You can earn money and recognition by writing articles and books for this hungry market. You can draw on your own and other people's knowledge and experience to write the kind of saleable material editors need.

Most magazines and newspapers publish how-to pieces. They might be clearly identified with titles like 'How to understand your cat', 'How to move house and stay sane', 'How to find the best value holiday' and so on, or they might appear under titles like 'Dress well for less', '101 ways to make housework fun!', 'Simple steps for beginning gardeners' and suchlike, headings which imply 'how-to' without actually using the label.

Bookshops are packed with titles on self-help, self-improvement, DIY, cookery, gardening, travel, business, finance and leisure, all aiming to help people improve their lives or achieve a goal they might not otherwise reach.

The how-to market has always been open to writers who can offer two essential qualities: knowledge of their subject and the ability to communicate that knowledge in clear unambiguous writing.

It's a particularly accessible market nowadays, with more people living longer in good health, and retiring earlier with time to do the things they've always wanted to do. People have also become more aware of their own physical and emotional well-being and are seeking guidance on how to look after themselves.

We all have skills, knowledge or personal experience that could be helpful to others. My first published article told how, with advice from the Royal Society for the Protection of Birds, my family protected to full fledging a pair of baby blackbirds fallen from an unwisely sited nest in our garden. The article was printed in a children's magazine with the sub-heading 'What to do if this happens to you'. By chance, I had written a how-to article.

A few years later I came across a small item in a writers' newsletter about a new publisher who was looking for suggestions for books to help people who wanted to develop new interests and possibly change their career path. With many years of experience in publishing, both in-house and as a freelance editor, I felt able to offer help to others who had ambitions to break into the world that had given me so much pleasure all my life. I sent the publisher a proposal for a book about getting published. He liked the idea, and my career took a new turn. That book was first published in 1989 and is still in print today, in its sixth edition, and is still a steady seller.

Since then, I've published many how-to articles, mainly on the craft of writing and the art of getting published, plus another three how-to books.

What skill, knowledge or experience do *you* have that might help other people? This book will show you:

- how to assess your knowledge, skills and experience
- how to organise what you know into saleable how-to writing
- where and how to sell what you write.

The easy to follow step-by-step approach is designed to show both the beginner and the more experienced writer how to write how-to material and get it published.

What you write could change someone's life. They might even write and tell you so.

# 1 You know more than you think you know

## What is a how-to?

A how-to is a piece of non-fiction writing—a tip, an article, or a full-length book—that explains to the reader how to carry out a specific task, achieve a specific goal or solve a specific problem.

More precisely, it's 'how-to-do-it' writing, but the shorter form is more concise and just as easily understood. It's a field of writing that is always open to fresh voices and new angles.

What makes good publishable how-to writing is not only an author's ability to explain *how* something should be done, but also their skill in explaining *why* the project or the problem should be tackled in a particular way.

There are two main types of how-to: practical/instructional ('how to make' and 'how to do'), and self-help/lifestyle ('how to live' and 'how to achieve'). We'll be looking closely at both types. For the moment, keep your mind open.

Every one of us has our own way of looking at the world. Your unique life experience will give your how-to writing a perspective and flavour like no one else's.

## Why write how-to?

You've heard the old cliché, 'Everyone has a book in them.' I believe this is true, but not in the sense that 'a book' means a blockbusting thriller or a bestselling romance. Success in fiction-writing needs a special blend of talent and determination plus a large measure of luck. I do believe, though, that anyone who has experienced the pleasures and coped with the problems that life throws at every one of us is capable of writing material that other people will value, and stands a far greater chance of getting published than writers who focus only on fiction.

Whether you're a seasoned writer or a complete beginner, the how-to field offers a fast track to publishing success. There is a huge and hungry market for how-to writing, from tips and fillers to articles and books. It's a market that is wide open to any writer who can supply the material editors constantly need to feed the public's insatiable appetite for advice. The demand never dries up.

How-to writing has a long history, and has inspired some of the world's best-selling and sometimes surprising books. *Mrs Beeton's Book of Household Management*, for example, and Dale Carnegie's *How to Win Friends and Influence People* are still selling strongly. The Dalai Lama is a prolific writer of how-to books; his published titles include *The Essence of Happiness: A Guidebook for Living* and *How to See Yourself As You Really Are.* Lynne Truss's million-selling *Eats, Shoots & Leaves: The Zero Tolerance Approach to Punctuation* took the publishing world by surprise. And who would have predicted chart success for Harry Mount's *Amo, Amas, Amat ... and all that: How to Become a Latin Lover.*

Today's readers want to be informed. They want to know about the latest medical breakthrough, what the smart set will be wearing next season, how to beat global warming, how to stretch time, how to find the best place to invest their money...

People are seeking their entertainment from sources other than reading—television, radio, films, music and now the internet, too. They're turning more and more to magazines and books for information and guidance on every imaginable aspect of living. From young people looking for advice on juggling their time and finances to older people taking advantage of better health and longer life, the readership for how-to articles and books embraces the whole population.

This hunger to be guided and informed is reflected in the popularity of spin-off books from television programmes like *You Are What You Eat* (how to eat well, feel better, and lose weight), *Property Ladder* (how to make money as a property developer), *What Not to Wear* (how to dress to suit your colouring and body shape) and *Grand Designs* (how to build your dream home). And let's not forget the 'Agony Aunt/Uncle'/ 'Ask Us Anything' section, still a staple of most popular magazines.

To see for yourself this explosion of interest, I would like you to go out armed with a notebook and pen and spend a few minutes in any large newsagents. Take any magazines other than the fiction 'specials' off the shelf and read the contents pages. Look at a variety of titles on different topics. Note the ratio of non-fiction to fiction. It's a pretty safe bet that you'll see far more articles than short stories. It's also highly likely you'll find at least one how-to piece, even if the words 'how to' don't feature in the title.

Most magazines publish no fiction at all. Yet if you ask any group of aspiring writers what they're working on, the answer from most of them will be short stories—by a long way the favourite—or novels of all recognised genres and none. By choosing to write non-fiction, especially how-to material, you're putting yourself ahead of these hordes of fiction writers, most of whom will never see their stories published.

### Make a note

- Most magazines publish no fiction.
- Your chances of publishing success are infinitely higher with non-fiction.

There are how-to pieces everywhere. Leafing through the glossy local 'shopping and entertainment' magazine on a recent holiday break, I found an article asking 'Why is it so hard to say what we really mean?' The only non-shopping, non-entertainment item in the publication, this self-help piece explained how to make sure that the words you speak convey the meaning you really want to communicate. Why was this article there? Who knows? Maybe the editor found herself with a blank page to fill, maybe she thought it would help her readers get better service in their hotel or book the best seats at the resort's summer show...

The financial section of my Sunday newspaper is packed with how-to pieces—a more obvious market than the one mentioned above. This week's selection tells me how to buy property in Bulgaria, how to choose the best value-for-money family holiday, how to look after myself on a continental camping trip, how to pack my holiday suitcase for a crease-free arrival, and how to not to fall out with my holiday companion.

### Make a note

- Weekend newspapers in particular use many how-to pieces.
- Look in the supplements for inspirational ideas.

Before you read any further, I would like you to go through any newspapers and magazines you have to hand—especially hobby and special interest magazines—and look for how-to pieces, from fillers and tips to full-length articles. Could you have written any of these?

And take heart from this: *The Writer's Handbook* lists almost 800 book publishers in the UK. Of these, more than 100 invite proposals for books in the how-to/self-help category, including more than 20 who want activity material for children. Fewer than 80 of the 800 publishers listed want fiction of any kind. When you consider the fact that at any given time many thousands of writers are competing to get a novel published, with only a 1 in 2000 chance of success—and that hasn't changed for decades—it isn't hard to see that as a writer of non-fiction you have a far greater chance of achieving your ambition.

Plenty of good reasons, then, to write how-to:

- There's a wide, varied and open market.
- You can earn good money.
- You don't need a track record to break in.

- You don't need an agent.
- Your work won't be consigned to the slush pile—you won't write your article till an editor shows interest, and you won't write your book till you have a contract with a publisher.
- Your successful how-to writing will give you credibility both in the writing world and with the public.
- You can start as small as you like, with how-to tips and fillers, or you can go straight to writing how-to articles or full-length how-to books.
- You'll never run out of ideas. Ideas are everywhere. They're inspired by every aspect of life. It's what you do with the idea that matters.

## Write how-to at any age

There are no age limits for writing how-to. You don't need to be young, glamorous or 'marketable'. What matters is the quality and saleability of the material you write.

If you've been thinking for a while about writing but are worried that you might be too old, too young or too inexperienced to start, how-to writing could be the ideal field for you.

Or maybe you've been trying to get short stories or a novel published, without success. Breaking in with how-to pieces will boost your confidence in yourself as a writer and will also prove to editors that you can write publishable material, even if it is in a different field.

You don't need a string of letters after your name or any other special qualifications to become a published how-to writer. If you can explain clearly how to do something, in words you would use when speaking to a friend, you can write how-to. What you need to be able to do is:

- Communicate what you want to say in clear, plain, unambiguous English.
- Organise your writing into a logical sequence that will make sense to your reader.
- Cut out waffle.
- Set out instructions and measurements clearly and precisely.
- Write with accuracy, brevity and clarity.

*Make a note*

- How-to writing gives you a fast track to publication.
- Age is no barrier to writing how-to material.

## Assessing your knowledge, skills and experience

We all have experience and skills gained from our years of living, however young or old we are. What seems commonplace knowledge and practice to you might be a revelation to your neighbour. You've probably forgotten just how much know-how you've absorbed through dealing with the problems, big and small, that life has thrown at you. Your coping strategies could provide valuable help to someone else.

Maybe you've overcome an emotional problem or a serious setback in health, or perhaps you're living with a disability. Could you offer advice to other people facing the same problems? Rather than writing as professional to client, which can feel intimidating, you could communicate on a person-to-person level. One writer I know launched her writing career in her sixties with an article packed with advice on how people with severe arthritis, like herself, could cope with and enjoy holidays abroad.

And in practical living, people have grown tired of mass-produced goods and are looking for individuality in what they wear and in what they put in their homes. More and more, they're looking for hand-crafted and individually designed wares. There has been a widespread resurgence of interest in, for example, knitting, sewing and handicrafts of all kinds, especially those that reflect our growing concern with 'green' living. This is the trend that inspired comedienne Tracey Ullman to publish a book—co-authored with Mel Clark—titled *Knit 2 Together: Patterns and Stories for Serious Knitting Fun.*

Before you start racking your brains for a subject to write about, take a minute to look at the scope offered by just a few of the markets open to good how-to writing—and you can add any of your own special interests to this list:

- Health and fitness.
- Cookery, food and drink.
- Home management, maintenance and improvement.
- Conservation.
- Raising children.
- Handling family problems, both practical and emotional.
- Coping with illness and bereavement.
- Emotional well-being.
- Gardening, both traditional and organic.
- Business and careers.
- Home-based business.
- Technology.
- Travel.
- Retirement.
- Crafts and hobbies.
- Sports.
- Collecting.
- Fashion and personal style.
- Personal and household budgeting.
- Self-improvement for men, women, young, old, middle-aged...

(This list is limited here only by space—for a fuller range of how-to possibilities, see the Topics List in the Appendix.)

Reading that list has probably stirred one or two ideas already, ideas that could quickly vanish into the great black hole of lost opportunities, so I would like you to start an ideas notebook right now. Write down any and every notion that floats into your mind, however vague or 'off the wall' it might seem. Don't risk losing a gem.

Resist the urge to start writing, though. We're going to explore your potential as a how-to writer—and you might surprise yourself.

### Make a note

- *Always* make an immediate note of any idea that occurs to you, however small or vague or silly. Don't risk losing anything. You might discard it later as worthless, but you won't know its value till you explore all its possibilities.

## Assessing your potential as a how-to writer

Let's look at the first of the two essential qualities we mentioned in the introduction: knowledge of your subject. We'll look at the writing process later.

A sound knowledge of your subject will give your writing that essential ring of authority. For effective how-to writing, you need more than a theoretical interest in your subject—or you need to know someone who does have the knowledge and whose expertise you can draw on (see Chapter 11).

It helps, too, if you have a reputation in your field. Have you written on your subject, perhaps in specialist publications? Have you given talks, held exhibitions, won prizes, been written about? While it isn't essential for success, the recognition factor can be influential in your dealings with editors.

Even if you have no record, though, the chances are high that you've acquired enough knowledge and experience of at least one subject to write about it.

Before you read any further, take time to explore and assess the topics you might write about. This exercise is based on a workshop on how-to writing I've led several times at the Writers' Summer School at Swanwick in Derbyshire and the Writers' Holiday in Wales at Caerleon. It's designed to give you an objective insight into your own potential as a how-to writer. It's simple to do, and can coax an amazing amount of information out of your memory, as many people have found who have taken part in the workshops. 'I can't believe I've done all those different things in my life' and 'I'd forgotten how much I knew—how odd!' are typical reactions.

You need four large (at least A4-sized) sheets of paper, plus pens or pencils.

Turn your pages to landscape, and, in a circle in the middle:

On sheet 1, write: What do you know?
On sheet 2, write: What have you done?
On sheet 3, write: What have you learned?

Use coloured pens or pencils, even crayons, to map out your answers. Playing with colour relaxes the brain by introducing

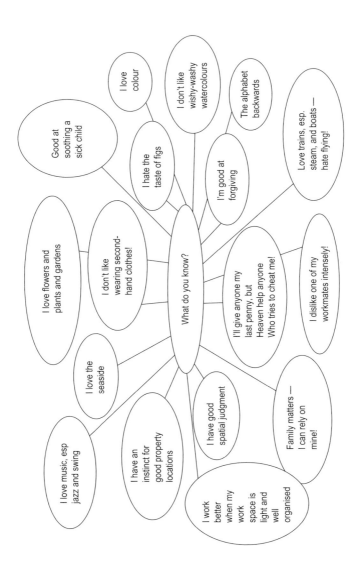

**Figure 1a: Self-assessment—What do you know?**

What do you know?

- Good at soothing a sick child
- I love colour
- I don't like wishy-washy watercolours
- The alphabet backwards
- I hate the taste of figs
- I'm good at forgiving
- Love trains, esp. steam, and boats — hate flying!
- I love flowers and plants and gardens
- I don't like wearing second-hand clothes!
- I'll give anyone my last penny, but Heaven help anyone Who tries to cheat me!
- I dislike one of my workmates intensely!
- I love the seaside
- I love music, esp jazz and swing
- I have an instinct for good property locations
- I have good spatial judgment
- Family matters — I can rely on mine!
- I work better when my work space is light and well organised

an element of playfulness to the exercise. This helps us to loosen up and forget our inhibitions.

I suggest the third person 'you' rather than the first person 'I' because this will encourage you to stand outside yourself and think objectively rather than subjectively. You *could* do the whole exercise on one sheet, but doing it in three separate sections helps you to alter the focus and stimulates different memories and perspectives.

Use the brain-storming technique known as 'Mind Mapping'—it's far more effective than compiling linear lists. Here's how to do it:

Settle down in a comfortable seat at a table. Place Sheet 1, 'What do you know?', on the table. Take a few moments to relax both your body and your mind. Let your tensions and inhibitions fall away. What you are going to write is between you and the page—no one else is going to read it. There is no score and no judgement. You can write about how you've always hated your brother or about the packet of sweets you pinched from Woolworth's when you were a kid or how you lust after your best friend's partner—no one will know.

Give yourself ten minutes only. Set a timer, if you can. The tight time limit makes you concentrate on trying to fill the page fast. Don't try to analyse what you write. Don't think about your responses. Just get your thoughts down on paper. Never mind if they seem either trivial or so huge that writing them down makes you uneasy. This is strictly between you and the paper.

### Make a note

- In an exercise like this, you need to shed your inhibitions to get the full benefit.
- Analyse nothing at this stage.

So—what do you know? As your first thought comes up, draw a line from the central question outwards like a branch of a tree, make a circle at the end of the branch and write your thought in the circle. Continue with other branches, other thoughts. Draw twigs from the branches, if you need them. Use wiggly lines, other shapes instead of circles—just relax and have fun.

Carry on till you've either run out of responses or your time is up. (See the example in Figure 1a on page 9.)

Put Sheet 1 aside, face down. Give yourself a break, take a walk or have a cup of coffee. You need time to clear your mind before you move on to the second question. Then take Sheet 2, and answer the question 'What have you done?' in the same way, again with a time limit of ten minutes. (See Figure 1b on page 12.)

Don't look back at Sheet 1. Some of your answers might coincide with or even duplicate your responses to the first question. Don't think about that. Just go on brain-storming till you run out of answers or time, then put Sheet 2 aside and take another break.

Come back to the exercise and apply the same technique to 'What have you learned?', again without thinking about your responses. (See Figure 1c on page 13.)

## Finding your most saleable topics

On your fourth sheet of paper, again turned to landscape, write five headings: 'Know', 'Done', 'Learned', 'Potential', and 'Market'. Then spread sheets 1, 2 and 3 out and link answers that appear to connect across all three sheets, however vaguely. Use coloured arrows to make your links clear. Note these answers, just as you first wrote them, on your fourth sheet under the corresponding first three headings. (See Figure 1d on page 14.)

As an example: If a reference to some aspect of coping with a sick child appears on each sheet, the first possibility you see might be something like that shown at the top of Figure 1d. Here you have a possible how-to article on looking after a sick child in a stressful situation. This could be either a general article or could focus on one particular aspect of the problem. Note down as many possibilities as you can think of under your fourth heading, 'Potential'.

Looking at something totally different in the second example, suppose you find you've referred frequently to your gardening skills—or lack of them: There is potential here for a humorous piece where you point out your own and possibly others' mistakes that have led to disastrous results, while at the

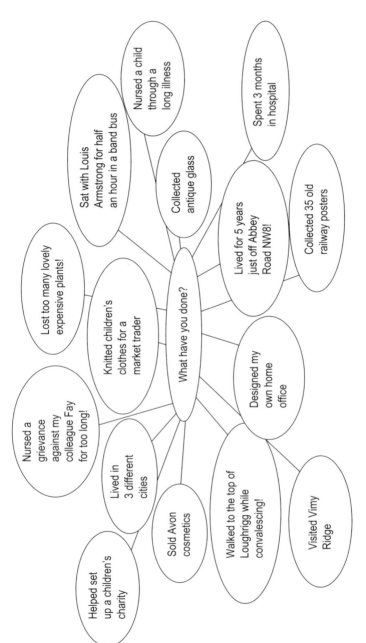

**Figure 1b: Self-assessment—What have you done?**

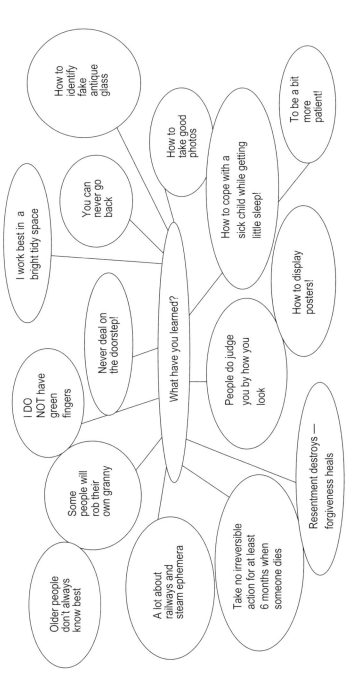

**Figure 1c: Self-assessment—What have you learned?**

| KNOW | DONE | LEARNED | IDEA | TYPE | MARKET |
|------|------|---------|------|------|--------|
| How to soothe a sick child | Nursed a child through a long Illness | How to cope with a sick child while getting little sleep | 6-point list to help worried parents to cope | Practical mini article | Parenting mag? Newspaper supplement? Women's mag? |
| I love plants and flowers and gardens | Lost a lot of very expensive plants | I do not have green fingers | How not to do as I've done! | Practical tips? Humorous piece | Gardening mag? Saturday mag? With practical tips? |
| I dislike my colleague Fay intensely | I've been nursing a grievance against Fay for months —I believe she stole my ideas! | Resentment destroys— forgiveness heals | How to get on with work colleagues you don't like Air-clearing advice? | Self-help narrative plus practical tips? | Women's mag? Saturday mag? Business mag? Newspaper Work Supplement? |
| I like to work in a bright well organised space | Designed my own home office | I work better when my surroundings are light, bright and orderly | How to design your own home office | Practical self-help | Business mag? Newspaper supplement Interior design mag? |

Figure 1d: Summarising possible ideas.

same time giving some practical instruction on how to avoid the problems.

With each connection you find, make a note in column four of every potential type of piece you might write from this single topic: tip, filler, article, possibly even a book…

Any subjects appearing on all three of your brain-storming sheets will offer the strongest potential for working up into sale-able material. Topics appearing on two out of the three sheets could also offer possibilities. (You can go on adding thoughts and ideas to all your sheets at any time—no one is watching!)

In column five, note possible markets. Be specific. Name any magazines you can think of that might be interested in the topic, any publisher who might be a prospect for a book proposal.

### Make a note

- Train your writer's brain to think 'markets' every time you identify an idea. Writers who are market-wise are the most successful.

From your results lists and your analysis on the fourth sheet, choose the topic you think would be of most interest and benefit to other people. Keep this topic in mind as you read on, and note any ideas as they strike you. Don't start writing the piece yet, though—it's enough for the moment to let the subject mature in your mind.

If you can't decide between two or more topics, choose the one you feel most enthusiastic about. Enthusiasm and the energy it generates are especially important if this is your first attempt at writing a how-to. There's a lot of work ahead, and you don't want to risk getting bored and running out of steam.

When you've decided on your subject, file your four sheets safely. How-to is an inexhaustible field, and you're sure to want to mine your notes for future pieces.

## The different types of how-to writing

Most how-to ideas fit into one of two main categories:

- Practical/instructional—how to make/how to do
- Self-help/art of living—how to live/how to achieve

Be clear in your own mind what kind of how-to you're going to write before you begin to refine your ideas and collect material. The different types demand different treatments.

### Practical/instructional

Here are a few examples of this type of how-to article from the pile of magazines by my desk at the moment:

- 'Create nesting sites to attract birds to your garden'
- 'Twenty-one ways to clear that clutter'
- 'Ten top tips on car maintenance'
- 'How to house-train your puppy'
- 'Six easy-to-make party cakes'
- 'Picture-perfect—how to take great holiday photos'.

Practical/instructional articles need down-to-earth, straightforward treatment. Your reader wants clarity. He doesn't want an elegant essay on the motor car or a treatise on green gardening—he wants to know how *he* should do it. He wants you to take him by the hand and guide him through the project, step-by-step.

Ideally, you should be able to groom the dog, cook the meal, build the patio … so that you can tell or show the reader exactly how to produce the desired results and how to avoid possible problems. If you don't have direct experience, interview someone who does, and ask them to check your copy before you pitch your article to an editor.

### Self-help/art of living

Again, a few examples from my own recent reading:

- 'Secrets of positive thinking—how to become a more confident person'
- 'Simple tips for coping with a panic attack'
- 'Going solo after years of marriage'
- 'Dress well for less—secrets of charity-shop shopping'
- 'Ten ways to put the sparkle back into your relationship'
- 'How to keep the family peace at Christmas'.

With self-help writing (how to live/how to achieve) people respond best to a style that is authoritative without being patronising, practical but not dogmatic. You need to find the most appropriate balance in the tone. There's a wide range of forms to choose from. We'll look in detail at different formats for each type of how-to in Chapter 5.

The market for how-to books is equally buoyant and varied. A glance along the shelves of your nearest bookshop will show you the wide range of possibilities. Here are a few examples:

### Practical/instructional

- 'Learn to paint abstracts'
- 'Recognising birds—a practical guide'
- 'How to knit simple garments for children'
- 'Collecting modern first editions'
- 'Upholstery for beginners'.

### Self-help/art of living

- 'Change your job, change your life'
- 'Living and working in France'
- 'Eat well and live longer'
- 'Living with bone-pain'
- 'Managing your time—how to make the most of every minute'.

Next time you're in a bookshop, spend some time browsing the non-fiction shelves for possible ideas. Don't forget to take your notebook.

## Starting to build your files

If you're an experienced writer, you'll already have books and articles on subjects that interest you. Maybe you have files already. If you're a beginner, you'll need to start building files. Keep clippings and notes of anything relevant, however oblique the connection. Don't forget to record your sources. Editors might ask you where you got your information, and you'll need contact addresses if you want to ask for permission to quote published material.

### Make a note

- Always keep a note of sources and publication dates of research material. You might be asked to supply this information.

Keep your research scrupulously up to date. Readers won't appreciate information that's out of date, and your editor won't enjoy dealing with complaints.

Get your name on the mailing lists of manufacturers, businesses, clubs, associations—any possible source of information on your special subjects. Read your junk mail. It isn't always useless rubbish. You might find useful leads there.

If you need information about countries outside the UK, the relevant embassies and consulates will usually be happy to supply what you need, possibly including photographs if what you write is going to help promote their country in some way.

Use the internet judiciously. It's a goldmine of information on every subject you can think of, but do not rely on it as your sole source. (See the sections on 'Research' and 'Researching on the internet' in Chapter 9, where you'll also see how to organise your material.)

The next chapter gives you an overview of the way publishing works today. You need to know your way around or, like a tourist dropped in the middle of London without an A–Z, you could all too easily take a wrong turning, blunder down a blind alley, or even fall among thieves and lose your wallet.

Before you move on to Chapter 2, check that you've made a note of the important points as suggested, and that you've completed the exercises. You'll want to refer back to those exercises—they are there to provide a bank of ideas for expanding your career as a how-to writer.

## Points to remember

- How-to writing is non-fiction writing.
- Your life experience is unique, and has value to other people.
- How-to writing is always in demand.
- Your chances of getting your how-to writing published are high.
- You're never too young or too old to write how-to.
- The range of how-to subjects is huge.

# 2 How to survive and succeed in today's publishing world

## The relationship between writers and publishers

There are three facts you need to understand and accept if you want to be a published writer:

1. Publishing is a hard-headed and highly competitive business.
2. Publishing companies are not charities—they are not there to please and accommodate aspiring writers (other than 'vanity' publishers, of which more later).
3. There are many more unsuccessful writers than successful ones.

Before you start to write and market your how-to material, you need to have at least a basic knowledge of the publishing world. I'm placing this information early in the book so that you'll be aware from the start of how the relationship between writers and editors or publishers works. You should not venture into this business as a dreaming amateur. If you do, you'll be inviting disappointment and frustration.

However, if you're prepared to take a professional attitude to the business from the start, and are willing to work hard to achieve your ambition, you can take hope and encouragement from these facts:

- Good writers are an essential part of publishing. Without them, magazine editors and book publishers would be out of a job—there would be nothing for them to publish.
- You can learn how to study the market so that you can offer editors the kind of material they want—and, most importantly, not waste their time and yours by offering material they don't want.
- By writing well and presenting your work to the right market in an appropriately professional way, you'll put yourself ahead of the 95 per cent of hopeful writers who don't bother to learn how the business works.
- The writers who get published are not necessarily those who write the most brilliant manuscripts—they are the ones who take the trouble to learn how to please their target editors.

### Make a note

- Adopting a professional attitude from the outset will give you a head start over the competition.

## What it takes to be a successful how-to writer

Above all, you need to be focused on success and ready to learn. The next most important attribute is not, as you might reasonably think, the ability to write wonderful prose. Thousands of brilliant writers turn out beautifully written short stories, novels, articles and non-fiction books every year. Most of them will never get their work published. Why? Because they don't understand and are not prepared to take the trouble to learn what people actually want to read. This is probably the most important advice for any aspiring writer: *Write what people want to read.*

Let me give you an example: At a writers' forum held during a recent conference, a delegate asked the panel of experts on the platform why the articles she was sending regularly to a particular magazine kept getting rejected. She couldn't understand this because, she told us, '... the work I'm sending is so much better written than the stuff they're publishing every week.'

The magazine editor on the panel asked the writer which publication she was trying to break into, and was given the name of one of the most successful magazines ever published in the UK, a magazine whose every issue sells more than a million copies and whose editor has been lauded as 'Editor of the year' so many times we've all lost count.

As the panel expert pointed out, this would-be writer was making one of the most common mistakes. She assumed that she knew better than the editor how to please his readers.

If it had been deliberately staged, there could not have been a better example to show the assembled writers the importance of analysing and understanding the market you want to write for.

### Make a note

- Don't assume that you know more about a magazine's readers than its editor does.
- Write what people want to read.

In book publishing houses, especially in large ones, the final decision about whether a book gets published or 'returned to sender' is made these days by accountants, not by editors.

Editors select manuscripts from those sent in by agents, and occasionally find something worthwhile in the slush pile. They might then seek the opinion of an outside reader, often an expert in the book's subject. However positive that reader's report might be, and however highly the editor rates the submission, he or she still has to convince the company's accountants that the book will make money. A book's potential to enhance the publisher's profile and reputation is not enough nowadays. If it looks like a financial risk, it will be turned down. The accountants hold the purse strings and they have the final say.

### Make a note

- Your book has to be commercially viable to stand a chance of acceptance.

If you subscribe to any of the writers' magazines (and you should), you've probably read letters from unhappy writers complaining that publishers 'won't give new writers a chance, but don't mind publishing books by and about 'mindless celebrities'. What these moaners don't seem to realise is that the chart success of the new Jamie Oliver, Posh Spice or Katie Price provides the profits that allow publishers to take an occasional chance on an unknown writer. A year without a big seller can leave a large publishing house with no money to spare for a gamble.

Smaller publishers can be more flexible. They don't have the huge overheads and staff costs to meet, or a bunch of unforgiving shareholders to please. And sometimes they strike lucky, as Profile Books did with *Eats, Shoots & Leaves*. Your how-to book might stand a better chance with a smaller publisher than with any of the big conglomerates.

### Make a note

- Don't complain about big names getting published. The profits they generate might provide the cash that gives your book its chance.

## Getting your work considered for publication

Editors and agents seldom have time to sit down and read every manuscript that arrives on their desk. More often than not, they don't read beyond the first page, possibly even the first paragraph, before reaching for a rejection slip and your sae. 'Unfair!' you might cry? Not so. The great bulk of unsolicited work received in publishing offices is poorly written, badly presented, and more often than not has been sent to the wrong market anyway.

It's an old saying but a true one: 'You can only make a first impression once.' A publisher or editor assessing material submitted in the hope of publication is making a commercial decision. They will be investing their own, or their company's, money in you, and they will only do that if they believe that their investment has an excellent chance of generating a profit. Don't damage your chances by submitting a manuscript that is less than the best you can make it. Sending sloppily presented work is like turning up for a job interview in grubby clothes.

Check and double-check that you're sending your work to an appropriate market. The *Writers' & Artists' Yearbook* and *The Writer's Handbook* give a lot of information on what editors and publishers want and what they don't want. For magazines, though, this is only a starting point. There are no shortcuts. Nothing can replace hands-on analysis and close study of your target publication (see page 39).

### Make a note

- Only send your work to appropriate markets.
- Prepare and present your work to the highest professional standard.
- Persevere, but don't be a pest.

## It's not rejection, it's business — why work is turned down by editors

The word 'rejection' should have no place in a writer's vocabulary. The dictionary definition (Chambers) begins: 'To throw away; to discard; to refuse; to renounce …' Terms like these are not appropriate to the process of writing and submitting work for publication. The universal use of the word and the surfeit of advice this spawns gives it far too much weight in the minds of aspiring writers, many of whom lack confidence anyway. Fear of rejection looms so large in many writers' minds that they never send their work out anywhere.

Many a talented hopeful whose first offering flies back home trailing a 'Thanks but no thanks' compliments slip gives up there and then.

Please understand this: an editor's refusal to accept the work you've offered, be it article, non-fiction book, short story, novel, poem or any other kind of writing, is *not* a rejection. It's a business decision. You need to accept from the outset that not every piece of writing you send out is going to delight every editor you send it to—life is not like that. Magazine and book publishing companies are businesses—they do not exist to make writers happy.

You might be given a reason why your offering has been turned down, or you might not. You could beat yourself up for days, you could wallow in self-pity, or you could write the editor a nasty letter. (Fine, but please don't send it. The publishing world is small and loves gossip—you could get yourself black-listed.)

Or you could take a cool professional attitude, respect the refusal as the commercial decision it is and ask yourself frank questions about the quality of what you sent and about your marketing strategy. And then move on.

### Make a note

● An editor's decision to refuse work you've offered does not mean she doesn't like you. It's not personal. It's business.

## Learning to cope when your work is refused

If you've had your submission refused by your target market, here are a few questions to ask yourself—answer them honestly and they could help you get accepted next time.

If your target was a magazine or newspaper:

1. Was your submission as good in every way as you could possibly make it?
2. Was your manuscript crisp and clean and presented in the standard format?

3. Did you check that you were sending your work to an appropriate publication, correctly addressed to the appropriate person?
4. Did you check that your target market was currently open to freelance submissions?
5. Did you check that you were not targeting a slot usually or exclusively written by in-house staff?
6. Did you follow your target market's preferred submission procedure?
7. Did you make a comprehensive study of your target market?
8. Did you check all the facts and sources you cited?
9. Did you write in your target publication's preferred style, tone and language?
10. Was your piece an appropriate length?
11. Did you check your spelling, grammar and syntax thoroughly?

If you're happy with your answers to all these points, then you should accept that your work was probably returned for one of these reasons:

- The magazine might have a similar piece already in the pipeline.
- They published something similar between the time your piece was posted and the time the editor got round to reading it—if publication was any earlier than that, then you haven't been up-to-date enough in your market research.
- There has been a change of editor or editorial policy, too recent to have shown up in the issues you studied—this is sheer bad luck.
- Perhaps the editor simply didn't like what you sent—bad luck again. Another editor might love it.

### Make a note

- If you're offering an article, it's wise to pitch your idea in a query to the editor before you actually write the whole piece—a brief 'No thanks' to an idea doesn't hurt quite so much.

If your book proposal is turned down, ask yourself:

1. Did you send it to a publisher who handles that kind of book?
2. Did you follow their stated guidelines for submissions— initial enquiry by e-mail, preliminary letter, covering letter plus proposal, covering letter plus proposal plus sample chapters … or whatever they asked for?
3. Did you address your enquiry or your proposal to the appropriate editor by name, correctly spelled and at the correct address?
4. Did you present your proposal like a professional, immaculately set out, with no typos or grammatical errors, and with every detail clearly expressed and unambiguous?

If you can answer 'Yes' to all the above, you've done your best and it's probably just a question of perseverance. Remember that you don't have to work your way through your list of possible publishers one by one. It's acceptable these days to send out your proposal to as many publishers as you wish all at once. Your writing life is too short to wait for months for someone to respond.

If you do this, and more than one publisher expresses an interest in meeting you, or asks to see more of the book, consider calling an agent and asking if they would be interested in representing you—they might be able to get you a better deal.

## 'Vanity' publishing—what it is and why you should avoid it

You've probably seen their adverts in magazines and in the national press and perhaps also (shamefully, in my view) in writers' magazines. You might even have been tempted by their siren call: 'Writers! Send us your manuscripts. All subjects considered', 'Authors! Do you have a book that deserves to be published?' and so on. Such enterprises are called 'vanity' publishers simply because they pander to the vanity of writers who are so convinced of the worth of what they write that they are willing to pay money—sometimes many thousands of pounds—to satisfy their ambitions. (Sometimes these companies attempt to disguise themselves under the label 'Subsidy publishers', but it's essentially the same thing.) They can look pretty tempting, especially if that novel you've been working so hard on for years has just been turned down for the umpteenth time.

Don't even think about it!

Reputable publishers never advertise for manuscripts. They don't need to. They are inundated, every single one, with manuscripts pouring into their offices from all over the country, indeed from all over the world. Piles of manuscripts stand on their floors, teeter on their desks … Why would they ask for more?

When a regular publisher chooses a book to add to his list, he does so by a very careful process of selection. Every proposal and every manuscript must be thoroughly assessed, because the publisher is putting both his money and his reputation on the line. (That is why your book contract will contain a clause stating that the finished manuscript you supply must be 'acceptable' to the publisher. This condition allows him to refuse to accept the finished work if it doesn't live up to your proposal.)

The publisher bears all the costs involved in producing your book. In most cases, he will pay you an advance against royalties. He will arrange all the editing, printing, production and marketing. He takes all the financial risks.

### Make a note

- Publishers consider all book proposals and manuscripts very carefully.
- Your finished manuscript must deliver what you promised in your proposal. The publisher always includes a 'get out' clause in the contract.

And what does the vanity publisher risk? Absolutely nothing. You pay all his expenses up front, and he has no reputation in the business anyway. The vanity publisher has no selection process. He never turns anyone down. He'll give you no editorial assessment or input; your work will appear on the page exactly as you send it, complete with typos. The small print in the contract he gives you will only commit him to binding a very small number of copies, with further copies to be bound only when orders are received. And where are those orders going to come from? His name is known everywhere in the business, so no one will review your book, no bookshops will order it, and you'll be left to do all the selling yourself. You will lose your money.

If you would like to know more about the dangers of dealing with vanity publishers, contact Johnathon Clifford, who has campaigned tirelessly for years against these sharks and the damage they do. Johnathon will be happy to send you an information pack, either by post or by e-mail. See under 'Useful addresses' on page 217.

### *Did you know?*

Everybody wants to be a writer. Abraham Lincoln had a short story, *The Trailor Murder Mystery*, published in the 15th April 1846 edition of the Quincy, Illinois, *Whig*; the story was reprinted in *Ellery Queen's Mystery Magazine* in March 1952. Screenwriter Joe Eszterhas tells us in his book *The Devil's Guide to Hollywood* that Franklin Delano Roosevelt pitched a treatment for a screenplay to Paramount when he was a young man. If only one of these great men had written *How to Be a Good President...*

## Points to remember

- Publishing is a business and requires a businesslike attitude.
- To succeed, you must act like a professional from the start.
- Write what editors want, not what you think they should want.
- When an editor turns down your work, there is no personal animosity involved—it's a business decision.
- Do not *ever* consider 'vanity' publishing.

# **3** **Writing for magazines**

## The long tradition of how-to writing

The how-to article has been a staple of magazine publishing for as long as there have been magazines.

The most famous cookery writer in history, Mrs Beeton, began by writing articles for her husband Samuel's publication *The Englishwoman's Domestic Magazine.* In 1861, these articles were published in one volume as *The Book of Household Management Comprising Information for the Mistress, Housekeeper, Cook, Kitchen-Maid, Butler, Footman, Coachman, Valet, Lady's Maid, Laundry-Maid, Nurse etc etc* ...You might not have Mrs Beeton's advantage of being married to a publisher, but keep in mind the possibility that you might eventually publish a collection of your own articles.

### *A few examples*

Copies of *Housewife* magazine from the 1940s, found recently at a book fair, include these articles:

- 'We adopt a child—A mother with an only child of her own tells how she successfully adopted another baby'.

This piece is supported by a substantial sidebar headed 'How to adopt a baby', giving practical advice and listing contact addresses.

- 'Hold it!—Photography without tears'.
- 'Furnishing in wartime—Encouraging advice on the subject of setting-up house on a limited budget'.
- 'First Aid for Food Budgets'.
- 'Planning your dream house'.

Pick up almost any magazine today, of any type and subject, and you'll find at least one how-to piece. More often than not, it will have been contributed by a freelance.

Here's a selection of article titles from recent magazines:

- 'How to move house and stay sane'.
- 'How to make money working from home'.
- 'How to understand women through their cats'.
- 'Snack all day and lose weight'.
- 'Ten ways to banish a bad mood'.
- 'Twenty ways to boost your toddler's confidence'.

Wide and receptive as the how-to market is, though, you need to keep ahead of the competition by dealing with editors in the most professional way possible. The writing world has always been full of people who think that all they have to do is put fingers to keyboard and grateful editors will immediately reach for the chequebook. They are wrong.

This is a passage from the opening of a book titled *The Lure of the Pen*, written by Flora Klickmann, editor of *Woman's Magazine* and *Girls' Own Paper*. The author gives us an insight into why she buys only a small number—about six hundred—from the nine thousand submissions she receives every year. Most submissions are declined 'for one of three reasons; either,

'They are not suited to the policy and the requirements of the publishing house, or the periodicals, for which I am purchasing. Or,

'They tread ground we have already covered. Or,

'They have no marketable value.

"The larger proportion of the rejected MSS come under the last heading. They are of the "homing" order, warranted to return to their starting point.'

One of the earliest how-to books for writers, *The Lure of the Pen* was first published in 1919. And nothing has changed. Every editor working today would echo Flora Klickmann's lament.

### Make a note

- Look out for this book in second-hand book shops and at book fairs. It's packed with wisdom that doesn't date.

## The different types of magazines

The magazine market is huge—and increasingly competitive. Millions of pounds are invested every year in new launches, and eye-watering sums of money as well as many jobs can be lost when a title folds.

Magazines fall roughly into these categories:

- National, with a UK-wide circulation (*Tatler, Good Housekeeping, Country Life, Take a Break*).
- Country-specific (*The English Garden, Scottish Field, Ireland's Own*).
- County-specific (*Cheshire Life, Devon Life, Dorset Life, Cumbria Magazine*).
- Special interest (*Car Mechanics, Disability Now, Fishing News, Railway Magazine*).
- Professional (*The Lancet, Legal Week, Justice of the Peace*).
- Business and trade (*The Grocer, Retail Week, The Bookseller*).

Business magazines can be a lucrative outlet for the observant writer. A friend of mine sold a how-to article about moving house to a building society magazine, earning a higher than average fee.

Look beyond the usual reference books. You'll find many business, trade and professional publications listed in *Willing's Press Guide*. This is one to consult in the reference library. (The full three-volume set costs around £400.)

**Make a note**

- Use your initiative. Look at sources of information other than the usual yearbooks. There are hundreds more magazines published in the UK than are listed there.

## Selecting your market

Before you write a word, you need to find out if the magazine you would like to contribute to actually uses any freelance work. You'll be wasting your own and the editor's time if you send material, or even a query, to a publication that is entirely written by staff or by specialist writers.

Somewhere in nearly every magazine, often but not always in the masthead, you'll see a notice stating their policy on unsolicited submissions. For example, in an issue of *SHE* current at the time of writing, this notice states (in 'pass me the magnifier' print): '*SHE* is unable to consider unsolicited material for publication, cannot return it if submitted, and accepts no liability whatsoever for safe custody thereof.' Look up the entry for *SHE* in the 2008 edition of *The Writer's Handbook* and you'll read: 'Approach with feature ideas in writing or e-mail … No unsolicited material.' To the uninitiated, these statements might seem to contradict each other, but in fact they are both telling potential contributors that the editor won't look at uninvited manuscripts but will look at query letters.

In contrast, a recent edition of *Take a Break* states: 'We welcome letters, unsolicited manuscripts and photos, which should be sent with an sae, on the understanding that we cannot be held responsible for their safe custody or return.' In other words, they'll look at anything you like to send them, and there's no need to send a query before submitting material.

**Make a note**

- The usual and accepted way to approach a magazine is to send a query, not a manuscript.

*The Writer's Handbook* and the *Writers' & Artists' Yearbook* can be useful for searching out markets. Bear in mind, however, that the research for these annual publications is done many months before they go on sale, so some of their entries will be out of date by the time you read them. Do not rely only on yearbooks, even the most recent editions. There is no substitute for the hard slog of studying the publications themselves. You should never submit work to a publication you haven't read, anyway. You need to know what standard of work they're publishing.

### Make a note

- Never send work to a magazine you've never read. You need to know what they do and don't publish, and need to be aware of their ethos and their style.
- Don't rely on reference books alone for markets—their information might be out of date.

## Learning to think like an editor

Imagine yourself in the editor's chair: you're working on an issue-in-progress of your monthly magazine for dog-lovers. This issue is scheduled for publication in four months' time. Your regular writers are working on their various columns, and several have already sent in their copy. You've commissioned several pieces from writers you can trust to deliver what you've asked for. You're looking for a 'personal experience' story to fill the last remaining slot. You turn to the pile of unsolicited submissions on your desk—maybe you'll be lucky enough to find a sparkling well-written piece from a brilliant new writer.

You spend an hour ploughing through envelope after envelope. What do you find? Short stories (you never publish them), poetry (you never publish it), a rant about the fouling of pavements, an irate letter from a would-be contributor whose article on sheep-shearing you've recently returned, a letter from a writer you've never heard of asking you to tell him what he should write for your magazine (too lazy to think up ideas himself?) … and so it goes on.

How delighted you would be to find a crisp clean manuscript on a topic that is sure to interest your readers, well written to the right length and accompanied by great photos.

You scratch your head and wonder why so many writers seem to lose all sense of logic when they try to market their work. The writer is looking for a buyer for her writing, whether it's a poem, a short story, an article or a full-length book. If she had made, say, a hand-stitched cushion, she wouldn't ask a baker or a bookseller to display it in his window, would she? Yet every working day postmen deliver hundreds of manuscripts to totally inappropriate editorial offices.

You reach for your list of tried and trusted freelance writers and start making calls.

### Make a note

- Before you send out any work, try to look at it objectively and ask yourself if the editor you're sending it to will *really* find it interesting and appropriate.

## Understanding editors' likes and dislikes

### What editors like

First impressions really do count. Editors respond well to

- Writers who demonstrate familiarity with the publication when they make their first approach.
- Concise, courteous, businesslike queries on topics relevant to the publication, whether by post or e-mail.
- Correspondence and submissions addressed by name (correctly spelled) to the appropriate contact.
- Crisp clean manuscripts set out in correct standard format (see pages 98–101).
- Crisp clean stamped self-addressed envelopes bearing adequate return postage.

### What editors don't like

- Uninvited telephone calls or personal visits—they are busy people working to tight schedules.
- Uninvited faxes—you could be blocking pre-arranged incoming material.
- Chatty rambling e-mails.

- Chatty rambling letters.
- Submissions of material irrelevant to their publication.
- Unprofessional-looking manuscripts typed in single or one-and-a-half line spacing, or in a fancy typeface, or in faint hard-to-read type, or on thin paper.
- No sae, or a tatty recycled one they're expected to seal with sticky tape.
- Cover letters asking them to give you a critique of the ms you've sent them. Editors are employed to fill their magazine with the best material they can find. It is not their job to teach you to write.

And what is the most common complaint editors make about the many unsuitable queries and unsolicited manuscripts they receive from freelance writers? 'I can tell from the first line that they've never read my magazine, never even bothered to pick up a copy,' they'll tell anyone who asks.

You are never going to be guilty of that, are you?

Of course, you'll meet people in writers' circles and at conferences who will brag that they never bother with market research. They just write their stuff, pack it up and send it off to whichever magazine they fancy might like it. The writer who adopts the 'scattergun' approach might strike lucky occasionally, but it's an amateurish and haphazard way to go about your business. Your success rate will be immeasurably higher if you target your markets with care and thorough preparation.

## Analysing a magazine

'Study the magazine' is probably the most common advice you've been given. Common advice it might be, but it's undoubtedly the best.

You've probably been reading magazines for years—as a casual reader. Now you need to read your target magazine as a writer, a writer who wants to sell work to the editor. Don't begrudge the time and effort you'll spend on this. The more you study the magazines in which you want to be published, the stronger will be your instinct for what the editors want.

The same advice applies to newspapers, too—they can be a fruitful market for the how-to writer.

Take a single issue of a favourite magazine and analyse it as a potential market. Write down your thoughts, impressions and conclusions as you do this. Look at these points:

1. Is this a new magazine? Or a well established one? Some magazines print a volume number, for example Volume 6 No 12 of a monthly magazine would mean the December issue in its sixth year of publication. Many, though, simply print the year and the week or month of publication. *The Writer's Handbook* and the *Writers' & Artists' Yearbook* print the foundation year of many of the magazines they list.

   A brand new magazine might be more open to new writers than an established one, where the editor will already have a tried and trusted 'stable' of freelance writers. (Longevity doesn't guarantee survival, though, as shown by the demise of long-time favourites like *Woman's Realm* and *Family Circle*.)

2. Study only a very recent issue. Don't try to cut costs by buying back issues from charity shops or making notes from old copies in your dentist's waiting room. Magazines can change radically and quickly. Editors move around from magazine to magazine, from company to company, and they take their particular values, likes and dislikes with them.

3. Look at the cover. What does it tell you about the magazine? What kind of readers is it designed to attract? What kind of picture appears there? What kind of features are promised by the 'shout' lines? Health and beauty? Sex? Relationships? Money? Travel? Fashion? Business? Politics? Hobbies? Other special interests? Who is it designed to attract? Men? Women? Both? Younger or older readers? Is the tone serious or humorous?

4. Read the advertisements from cover to cover. What do they tell you about the magazine's target readers? Their age group? Their spending power? Their leisure interests? Their health concerns? Do the ads promote catalogue fashion, lower or upper end of the high street, department store or couture? Do you see ads for stair lifts and

bathing safety aids? Baby wear, school wear, budget family holidays? You can learn as much about a magazine from the ads as you can from the material it publishes.

5. Look at the table of contents. This is where everything in the magazine other than advertisements is listed. What does it tell you about the kind of material the magazine carries?

You'll probably see bylines here, too. Do you recognise all or most of the names shown? If the magazine features a lot of big names, it might not be a good market for a newcomer. Some magazines run a column giving information about the contributors featured in that issue. This can give you clues about your chances of breaking in.

Some of the material might be written by staff members. Compare the bylines shown in the table of contents with the names in the masthead—see below—to see how much of the content is written in-house and how much might be bought from freelancers.

6. Read the editor's letter. Many magazines open with a message to the readers from the editor saying, in effect, 'Hello and welcome to my magazine …' Read this message carefully. What does the editor write about? What do her comments tell you about her personality? About the magazine's attitude, values and focus? What kind of writing style do you see here? Casual or formal? Warm or distant? You can get an instinctive feeling about the general tone of the publication from what the editor says and the way he or she says it.

7. Study the masthead, the list showing the names and functions of the magazine's staff. (If your target magazine does not show such a list, you'll have to find out the appropriate names by other means, perhaps from the writers' guidelines, if these are available, or from the website, or by phoning the switchboard and asking.) Some of the titles you're likely to find in the masthead are:

● Editor (sometimes Editor-in-Chief): The person in overall charge of the editorial content.

- Managing editor: The editor in charge of the magazine's publishing schedule.
- Features editor: The editor who commissions features and articles—usually the best person to address your query to.
- Associate editor/assistant editor etc: editors in lower positions who might or might not work with writers.

8. Most magazines have regular sections, known as departments, carrying items of interest in a specific area. Departments usually carry shorter—often much shorter—pieces than the main features and articles. You need to study several consecutive issues to identify the regular departments. What subject area does each department cover? Are they written by regular columnists or do they appear to use a variety of writers? How much of the content is written by staff (their names will usually appear in the masthead) or by freelance contributors?

9. Study the letters to the editor that the magazine publishes. What do they tell you about the typical reader's concerns, attitude to life, feelings about the magazine and so on. Do the letters include tips the writer believes would be useful to the magazine's general readership? If so, this might be a good place to break in with some tips of your own. Just because readers' letters are short, don't make the mistake of assuming they are easy to write. A successful letter has to be as carefully crafted as a longer piece of writing—possibly more so, because of the need for brevity.

10. Read the articles and note the following:

- How do the articles usually begin? With an anecdote? With facts and figures?
- Are there any sidebars?
- Are there any first-person pieces?
- Are there any seasonal pieces?
- How many articles could be classified as how-tos? (Remember, they might not use the term 'how-to' in the title.)
- How long are the articles?

11. You should have a good idea of the general language and tone from the editor's message, but it will pay you to analyse the magazine's language with a forensic eye. Looks like a bit of a chore? Yes, perhaps, but you're a professional, remember, and successful professionals leave nothing to chance. Let's take a really close look:

- How does the overall tone and style of the magazine strike you? Formal and serious? Warm and friendly? Chatty and informal?
- Does the text on the page/in the columns look heavy and solid, or is it broken up into sections, with plenty of 'air' on the page?
- How many columns are there to the page? How wide are the columns? A narrow column width demands short words where possible, to avoid having too many hyphens at the end of lines.
- Are the paragraphs short and sharp? Or long and dense?
- Are the sentences simple and straightforward? Or extensive and complex, with sub-clauses?
- Are the words short, simple and 'everyday'? Or do they have you reaching for a dictionary?
- Does the magazine use many photographs? Study the illustrative content closely—it can tell you a good deal about what the readership is looking for.

A thorough understanding of and 'feel' for the magazine's readership will be invaluable when you come to pitch your ideas to the editor. It will also help you decide if you would feel comfortable writing for this audience. This is important, because you could find it difficult to write naturally if you don't feel at ease with the publication.

Do the same exercise with at least another two issues, to make sure this market is right for you.

**Make a note**

- Thorough market study is vital for freelance success—it's time and effort well spent.

## Inside information: writers' guidelines

If your target magazine offers guidelines for contributors, either by post in return for an sae or on its website, get them and study them closely. They are designed to save time and trouble for both the editorial staff and for contributors. They tell you, for example, how the magazine likes to be approached, the right people to contact, how they like you to present your work, how far in advance you should submit ideas for seasonal material and so on. They should also tell you whether the magazine wants photographs, what format they prefer, how to submit pictures and so on. Don't regard the guidelines as a substitute for studying the actual publication, though. You still need to get your own feel for the magazine.

The guidelines often tell you what the magazine is not interested in. This will help you avoid the all too common mistake of offering material the magazine has never used and is never likely to use in the future.

## Inside information: the media pack

Most magazines produce a media pack. This is a package sent out to prospective advertisers giving detailed information about the magazine's circulation and, most usefully for a writer, its readership. The media pack analyses the average reader's income, social status, business or leisure interests and so on. This could either confirm your impressions of the publication from your own detailed study or give you reasons to rethink your conclusions.

You should be able to obtain a copy for yourself by calling the magazine's publicity or advertising department. (If the person you speak to asks why you want it, be honest and tell them you're a writer. Don't pretend to be a prospective advertiser—what would you say if they asked you about your company, the products you want to advertise, your annual turnover...?)

# Inside information: the editorial calendar

If you possibly can, get hold of the freelance writer's secret weapon, the editorial calendar. This might be included in the media pack, it might be on the website, or you might have to ask the publicity department for a copy. In the editorial calendar you'll find details of the planned features and the editorial focus for each of the forthcoming year's issues of the magazine.

For example, if the February issue is devoted to summer weddings, it will be packed with all things bridal, from features to advertisements: clothing for the bridal party, catering, entertainment, honeymoon destinations, tips on love and romance and the like. Given this information, you could pitch, say, a how-to piece on wedding speeches, or on being the best-dressed wedding guest, or on making the perfect cake, or on budgeting for the big day, or on finding the perfect honeymoon hotel ... and so on.

### Make a note

- Make it your practice to get hold of *and read* as much information about your target publications as you possibly can. You'll streak ahead of all the writers who can't be bothered to do this.

# Lead times and how to deal with them

Lead times are vital in magazine publishing. The lead time is the time between the initial planning of an issue and its actual publication.

Magazine editors work on several issues at the same time, with each issue at a different stage in its production. For example, in mid-May, the editor of *Pen-pusher's Monthly* might be checking the final proofs of the August issue, due in the shops in early July, while at the same time editing manuscripts for the September issue, finalising material for October and November, and commissioning special features for December's Christmas issue. Weeklies have much shorter lead times, quarterlies much longer. It's no use sending a query about a Christmas piece in October—the Christmas issue will be ready to go to press by then.

For weekly magazines, the lead time will be at least six weeks, sometimes longer. So the savvy writer gets in his seasonal ideas in plenty of time.

You can see, then, that there has to be a (sometimes considerable) time lapse between the arrival of your first approach and the editor's decision to accept your finished piece for use in a particular issue. Many writers seem to be unaware of—or are unwilling to accept—this delay, and insist on calling to demand a decision only a few days after their query has gone into the postbox.

Lead times for newspapers are much shorter—by definition, they look for news, and are put together only hours before appearing on the news-stands. However, the magazines you buy with your newspaper at weekends are little different from the weeklies, in that they need more preparation time than their parent newspaper. (That's why you might find a big celebrity wedding reported in the magazine, with lavish photographs and breathless commentary, and then read in the accompanying newspaper that the couple have already split up.)

A shorter lead time, though, does not mean that it's okay to pester the editor.

**Make a note**

- It's unprofessional to disregard lead times.

## Key strategies for a positive reaction

In the intensely competitive world of magazine publishing, editors seldom read right through every manuscript that crosses their desks. Apart from the constant pressure of time, most of the mss they're sent don't merit more than a cursory glance. Hard though it is to accept when you've sweated blood over your work, most editors scan only a paragraph or two, maybe a page at the most, before reaching for the standard rejection slip and your sae—unless your material really grabs their interest.

Here are some positive steps you can take to give yourself at least a chance of avoiding instant dismissal. Save yourself a lot of heartache by checking your submission against the following points before you send it out anywhere:

- Do print out your work in a plain serif font like Times New Roman, in 12 point size.
- Don't print your ms in any kind of fancy hard-to-read font, or in italics, or in condensed type. Editors won't thank you for straining their eyes or their patience.
- Do use only plain white A4 paper and black ink. (One editor I know keeps a 'horror file' of work she's been sent—I wish I could show you the stuff written on bright pink paper, on multi-squared graph paper, on the reverse of old manuscript pages, on the inside of the back of a cereal packet … Those are not exaggerations. I've seen them.)
- Don't present your work in faint print, squeezing every last drop from your ink cartridge or worn-out ribbon.
- Do leave adequate margins around your text (see page 98–9 for details of how to set out your ms).
- Don't justify (make even) the right-hand edge of your text—leave this edge ragged.
- Do set your text to double-spacing, ie, leave a full line of white space between lines of text. (Please note that double spacing does *not* mean leaving two spaces between words!)
- Don't try to get away with single or one-and-a-half-line spacing—a plea that you're helping to save the planet won't impress a busy editor.
- Do hit the space-bar only once after a full stop—word-processing programs automatically leave extra space here, so if you put in two spaces you'll cause an unacceptably wide gap between sentences.
- Don't pepper your manuscript with copyright symbols. This will tell the editor that you're a potentially trouble-some amateur.

- Do remember to put your name and address and contact details on your ms. Every publishing office, big or small, has a drawer crammed with unidentifiable submissions—make sure yours won't be one of those.

- Don't bind or staple your work. Use a simple paper clip for a short ms or a strong rubber band for a full length book ms.

- Do put a catchline at the top of every page showing, in an abbreviated form if necessary, your name, the title of your work, and the page number. For a full-length book ms, number the pages straight through—*do not* number each chapter separately.

- Don't rely on your computer's spellcheck facility—it won't pick up words that exist but are used wrongly, such as 'there' instead of 'their' or 'grime' instead of 'grim', 'principle' instead of 'principal' and the like.

- Do print your work out for that essential final check—you'll pick up errors far more readily than if you read on-screen.

These checks won't guarantee a sale, but they will encourage the editor to regard you as a professional and give your work a lot more than a quick glance.

### Make a note

- Make every piece of work you send out as good as you can possibly make it. Love your work—it's worth your care and attention.

Keeping in mind the advice and information you've read in Chapters 2 and 3, you're now ready to move on with confidence to writing and selling your first how-to pieces.

## Points to remember

- How-to articles have been popular in magazines for many years.
- There are magazines to suit every taste and interest.
- It's vital to choose your market carefully and study it well.
- Learn to look at your work from the editor's perspective.
- Take care to make a good first impression.
- Get as much information about your target market as you possibly can.
- Respect your target market's lead times.
- Make every aspect of your submission as professional as you can.

# Breaking in with tips, fillers and mini articles

## The potential for selling short material

In October 2006, *Writers' News* reported that in *The People* newspaper's gardening section the Letter of the Week won £25 with this tip: 'Bunches of lavender will keep flies out of your kitchen.' This ten-word 'how to keep flies out of your kitchen' tip earned £2.50 per word. How many other types of writing can you think of that pay a rate like that? I've made that kind of money writing humorous greeting cards, but that is a craft all on its own and is a lot more demanding in time and originality. (I once sold a how-to birthday card idea, though, to Hanson White; it read 'What's the best way to keep your youth? Lock him in the bedroom!')

Most of us are short of time and money. We're all looking for quicker, cheaper and more efficient ways of doing things, whether it's keeping the house on the civilised side of clean, finding ways to stretch the food budget or juggling childcare with a paying job.

Many magazines will pay you to share your know-how on saving time, money and energy. These might be tips or shortcuts you've worked out for yourself, been told about by a friend, or adapted and improved from something you've read. Many a time I've read a tip in a magazine and thought 'But my mother used to do that...'

As Alison Chisholm writes in her book *How to Write Five Minute Features*, 'When you think of an idea for a tip, you may react by saying to yourself: "There's nothing new in that—I've been doing it for years." And this is often the case. You must remember, however, that the little practices you have developed over a period of time and now do as a matter of habit are clever, original ideas for people who have never thought of them.'

Tips can range from the very simple and straightforward to the highly technical and specialised, depending on the market you want to break into. If you send useful tips regularly to your target publication, the editor will come to recognise your name, a big plus if you want to move on to offering longer pieces.

### A couple of examples

Big-selling magazines like *Chat* and *Take a Break* pay top money for tips. Many of these magazines fill a whole page, sometimes more, with tips—clearly, their readers love them. A tip plus a photograph earned £200 for showing how using a moist wipe and Coconut Oil Hairshine can polish up an umbrella plant—at eighteen words this works out at more than £11 a word.

Another tip showed how to secure a hose to a tap with elastic bands, to prevent spraying. Fifteen words, no photo, payment £30.

If you specialise in tips on a particular topic or a related range of topics, you could eventually publish them as a collection. Books with titles like *1001 Household Tips*, *How to Win Consumer Competitions* and *Strategies for Small Gardens* sell well. Keep this possibility in mind, and never throw anything away, whether it gets published or not.

### Make a note

- Writing tips is an effective way to get your name known to the magazine's staff.

- Success with tips could open the door to selling how-to articles in the future.

## Finding ideas for tips

When you tell someone you're a writer, one of the first things they'll ask you is 'Where do you get your ideas?' For the how-to writer, the answer is so obvious you wonder why everyone in the world isn't writing. You get your ideas from life. You could never run out of ideas if you lived a dozen lifetimes. In the next chapter you'll see how to generate a wealth of article ideas. Before that, though, tip-writing will get your how-to writing muscle toned up ready for more ambitious projects.

Get into the habit of looking objectively at every task you do in the home, in the garden, at work, at play, or in pursuing any of your special interests or activities. Keep a small notebook with you and write down anything that strikes you as being potentially useful as a time- or money-saver. You don't have to write the idea in detail, but you need enough words so you can remember why you thought it worth noting. A keyword might not be enough.

### Make a note

- *Always* write down the nub of an idea the instant it strikes you. You might think it's so brilliant you couldn't possibly forget it, but why take the risk?

Ideas can present themselves at any time. Take this 'something from nothing' example: Half-a-dozen of us were sitting round a table at a writer's conference, having a coffee break and cursing those little milk pots where you have to peel off the top to get the milk out. Someone said, 'It's a lot easier if you tilt the pot backwards at an angle while you open it—that stops the milk gushing out.'

'That's a good idea,' we all said. And a tip was born. We posed a fresh milk pot, tilted back between a thumb and a forefinger with the 'opening' action shown, took a photograph and scribbled a few words, all to be worked up at home (by the person who suggested the idea) into a tip that sold, with the photo, to a women's magazine—earning £30.

### Make a note

- Get a notebook and pen and go from room to room in your house noting down anything, however small, that you've found a different or better way of doing since you moved in.

### Turning a setback into an opportunity

We had a violent storm here yesterday. We were warned it was coming and we sat tight, hoping we wouldn't lose the roof. What we didn't do was go out and check the garden before the storm hit, to see if anything needed securing. This carelessness cost us a beautiful little willow tree, snapped above the roots by a vicious gust of wind. The strap holding it to its support stake had rotted, and we hadn't noticed. If only we had looked...

Taking a positive view, this experience offers an idea for a how-to piece, something on the lines of 'Storm Warning—protect your vulnerable plants and trees before the winds arrive'.

### Make a note

- When something goes wrong, put your writer's hat on and look for possible tip ideas.

Another useful way to find ideas is to listen closely when friends and colleagues mention any problems they're having, whether with practical living, relationships, money or anything else. Write them down (discreetly) in your ever-handy notebook. In your next writing session, list these problems, look at them objectively rather than from your friends' point of view, and see if you can come up with solutions.

The problem pages in magazines offer plenty of possibilities. How many times have you read an 'agony' letter and thought you could come up with a better suggestion for dealing with the problem than the one suggested by the columnist? The 'agony' business is the self-help world in miniature.

Ideas are everywhere. Start by making a list of everyday situations, activities and problems. You could draw on your responses to the exercises in Chapter 1 for this.

Take the most promising item on your list and, on a separate sheet of paper, give it the brain-storming treatment you used in the self-assessment exercises. Note down every angle and sub-topic you can think of that relates to the central subject, however remotely. Let your imagination run free—don't dismiss any fleeting thought, however zany it might seem. (A big plus with this kind of exercise is the way it encourages 'off-the-wall' thinking.)

You don't need to spend hours at a time on this—just fill a new balloon as another possibility pops into your mind.

### Ask a man (or woman) who knows

Another way to find tip ideas is to ask the advice of people who are deeply involved in some subject or activity. A bowling-green keeper, for example, could give you tips on keeping a lawn in good condition. A friend who makes her own clothes will know about mending seams and putting up hems.

Sources of good saleable tips are all around us. We just need to train ourselves to think about them.

### Make a note

- Write down the names of everyone you know who is accomplished in any activity and who might be a fund of saleable tips. (Don't pester people, though—you don't want to lose all your friends!)

## Suiting the tip to the publication

The way you write up your tip will depend on the market you have in mind. The same principles of market study we looked at in Chapter 3 apply to tips as well.

You have to write them up in the most appropriate form and language for your target market. Some magazines run specific columns for tips, others prefer to see them as readers' letters. Be alert to changes. Study current issues only—many magazines introduce new columns and drop old ones frequently, so don't waste your time—and the editor's—by sending your tip to a market that has changed or vanished.

Keep up to date with styles in which tips are laid out, too, especially if a new editor has taken over. New brooms like to make changes, sometimes just for the sake of it.

Keep your tips as concise as possible. Check the number of words in tips already published. Some magazines allow a more generous word count than others. Don't offer anything longer than the norm. A 100-word tip sent to a section that never uses anything longer than 50 words will be binned.

Set out your tip in the form your target publication currently uses. Here are three different ways to write the same 'green living' tip.

1. Begin with an imperative verb: 'Add a tablespoon of white vinegar to your wash cycle's final rinse instead of costly and environmentally harmful fabric softeners. Your laundry will feel as soft and smell as fresh.' (30 words)

2. Begin with a statement: 'Fabric softeners are expensive and might contain ingredients that could harm the environment. Use white vinegar instead, added to your final rinse cycle.' (23 words)

3. Begin with an adverb: 'When giving your laundry its final rinse, add white vinegar to soften and freshen. It costs less and won't harm the environment.' (22 words)

For practice, rewrite this tip in other forms, beginning with an infinitive, a conditional, a question, a summary statement...

Look through your favourite magazines for other forms, and practise writing your own tips to suit these markets. Use as few words as necessary to make your point in the appropriate style. It will pay you to practise this exercise—there's a lot of competition out there.

In some publications, each tip has a short title, usually two, three or four words. If this is the norm in your target publication, think up a title for your tip. For the tip idea in the examples above, you could suggest something like 'Soft but safe' or 'Soft, fresh and harmless'. Can you think of something better?

*Make a note*

- Tips relevant to 'green living' are growing in popularity. Tips on gardening in a low rainfall area, for example, are finding a ready market.

## Writing and selling fillers and short articles

The next step in your how-to writing is to move on from tips to fillers and mini how-to articles. These can range in length from around 100 to 500–600 words. You don't need to send a query to the editor before submitting these short pieces. A query would take as long to read as the piece itself. Simply send them in as you would a tip.

These short how-to pieces usually take the form of a couple of short introductory paragraphs summing up the purpose of the piece, followed by a series of tips on how to solve a problem or how to carry out a project. The tips are often set out as a series of numbered or bulleted points, rather than whole sentences. This form helps the reader to absorb the information more readily, while economising on space and wordage. (A cynic might suggest that it panders to the ever more prevalent 'thirty-second attention span syndrome'!)

Typical ideas for practical how-tos might be:

- 'Beat the clock—Ten Top Tips for Managing your Time'.
- 'Twelve Tips to Cut the Clutter'.
- 'Green gardening—a dozen ways to make a difference'.
- 'Handle cleaning products safely—six tips to protect you and your family'.

And for lifestyle pieces:

- 'How to deal with those noisy people next door—six ways to neighbourhood harmony'.
- 'Fun for the whole family—holiday harmony in six easy steps'.
- '"Are we nearly there?"—Keep the journey jolly with these great car games'.

- 'Good manners start at home—six simple ways to make family life a pleasure'.

Some publications prefer to start each point with a bold or italicised word rather than numbers or bullets. Whatever their preferred method, you'll increase your chances of success if you set out your material in their style.

Keep an eye on what's happening around you and on what is being reported in the news. In a recent example of a topical how-to, the children's newspaper *First News* carried a short piece following reports of a child being mauled to death by a dog. This consisted of a headline and three paragraphs, 63 words in all, followed by a box containing 32 words of advice on how to protect yourself if you think a dog might be about to attack you.

### Make a note

- Be alert to current concerns. Many publications welcome topical advice and solutions in the form of tips.

## Submitting short material

Don't bother sending a stamped addressed envelope with tips or fillers. Anything not used will be discarded. You won't know if you've been successful till you either see your tip in print or receive a cheque.

It's worth enclosing an sae with a mini article, though. You'll have a chance of getting your unused material back and can then send it out elsewhere.

## Keeping submission records

Start recording your submissions as soon as you send out your first offering, whether it's a tip, a filler or a mini article. By keeping track of everything as you send it out you won't forget when and where you've submitted either material or queries. You don't want to be draining your energy by fretting about where your stuff is and whether it's too soon to expect decisions. Good records will also safeguard against accidentally submitting the same material to an editor who has already rejected it, a less than professional thing to do.

You can set up a spreadsheet if you're using a computer, or log your submissions in a notebook. For tips and readers' letters where the reward is a prize, a simple record of what you sent, when you sent it and the market you sent it to will be enough. For article queries, you need to keep records that include any payments you receive—you'll need to declare these to the tax man (see 'Keeping financial records', below). Set up your system to record the following essentials:

1. The idea.
2. The magazine you've sent the idea to.
3. The editor's name, the submission address and e-mail address.
4. The date submitted.
5. The date by which you can reasonably expect a response.
6. The date you get a response or refusal, or see your work published, or receive a cheque.
7. The date you plan to follow up the query if you don't get a response.
8. The date the contract was signed, if appropriate.
9. The date you submitted your invoice, if you need to.
10. The date you received payment.

You can make these records as simple or as detailed as you wish, to suit your own needs.

## Keeping financial records

You need to keep precise records of every financial transaction connected with your writing, so that you can make an accurate declaration of your earnings to the tax man. You might not consider yourself to be a 'professional' writer, but the Inland Revenue requires you to declare every penny you earn—except for competition prizes, which are tax-exempt *at the time of writing this book.*

You are allowed to claim certain expenses against tax, though, so it's worth keeping all your receipts safely noted and filed. Allowable expenses include:

- Secretarial, typing, proof-reading and research.
- Telephone calls, stationery, computer and printer supplies.
- Periodicals, reference books and other printed material relevant to your business.
- Subscriptions to societies and associations relevant to your business.
- Travel expenses incurred in your business activities.
- Premiums to certain pension schemes.
- Accountancy charges and legal charges relevant to your business.
- Capital allowances for equipment—computers, printers and the like.

This is by no means a comprehensive list—the rules are constantly under review. It's worth getting a copy of the Society of Authors' *Quick Guide to Income Tax* which explains in detail the complexities of tax as it affects writers (see under Further Reading).

Letters, tips and other short pieces will tone up your writing muscle. With a bit of practice on these and your growing familiarity with the markets, you should be ready to move on to the bigger challenge of writing and selling how-to articles.

A tip for your comfort: To reduce eye-strain when you're working on-screen use the 'zoom' facility to increase the size of the visible type. This makes no difference to the actual type size; it only enlarges the way it looks. Look for the zoom in the drop-down menu under 'View' on the toolbar.

## Points to remember

- Your know-how can earn you good money for just a few words.
- You can train yourself to be alert to ideas.
- Every idea you think up has further potential.
- Every tip you send must be right for its target market.
- Good records avoid duplicating submissions.
- Good financial records keep the tax man happy.

# 5  Writing how-to articles

## If you can write, you can write how-to

Writing a successful how-to article that will interest, stimulate, encourage and help people is certainly within the capabilities of any competent writer. You don't need to be able to produce poetic prose. You don't need a vocabulary as big as the Oxford English Dictionary. You do need to be able to:

- write simple straightforward English
- sort information into a logical order
- convey your meaning to your reader in clear unambiguous language
- anticipate your reader's reaction to what you write—in other words, you have a responsibility to think carefully about any advice you offer.

People are hungry for advice and instruction in all areas of their lives. Give them the best you can.

### Make a note

- How-to writers will never run out of readers.
- To please those readers, you must give them the best advice and instruction you can, in the clearest possible way.

## Ideas galore!

As promised in Chapter 4, you need never run short of ideas. Perhaps you surprised yourself with the breadth and depth of your responses to the self-assessment exercises in Chapter 1. Now we're going to take those exercises to the next level, using the same brain-storming or 'clustering' method.

Working from the exercises as carried out by our exemplary writer, we'll focus on 'railways and steam trains'. Our writer is particularly interested in collecting all kinds of memorabilia from the age of steam. This material would be categorised in a collectables price guide as 'Railwayana'. If we brain-storm 'railway collectables', we come up with a wealth of topics like:

1. Ephemera—tickets, labels, postcards, cigarette cards, handbills, posters, advertisements
2. Stamps—railway and engine commemorative issues
3. Timetables, maps, guidebooks
4. Plates and nameplates
5. Uniforms, buttons, whistles, signal flags
6. Art—paintings and prints
7. Medals and awards
8. Pottery, china and silverware
9. Lamps and reading lights, including personal lamps and lapel candles
10. Emblems
11. Model engines, carriages, wagons, tracks, stations
12. Doorplates and shed plates
13. Clocks
14. Luggage…

Maybe you can come up with even more. So here we have fourteen connected yet different areas that would interest a collector, and every one of the fourteen is a possible article topic in its own right. As these are all sub-topics of the general subject 'Transport', you can see that there's a rich seam of possibilities in this area alone. How could anyone ever run out of ideas?

**Make a note**

- Get into the habit of brain-storming every how-to idea you can think of, and start ideas files. You never know when you'll spot an opening.

## Assessing your idea's value to the reader

Finding how-to ideas is easy, as we've shown above. However, before you expand any idea, you need to assess what kind of treatment of the idea would present the greatest benefit to your reader. When you're writing a how-to piece, there is little point in displaying how much you know about the topic if you don't also explain to the reader what he should look for if he wants to start collecting or dealing. Without the instructional angle, you might write an interesting piece, but it wouldn't be a how-to.

Let's look, then, in more detail at the first of these topics, railway ephemera, thinking now like a how-to writer. Brain-storming again, let's see what angles we can find here. You might see possibilities in:

1. How and where to buy and sell.
2. Is it genuine?—how to recognise a fake.
3. How to conserve, restore, and possibly repair these fragile items and protect them from damage by light or rough handling.
4. How and where to display a collection.

Any of these angles would work well as a how-to article.

When you're looking at ideas for how-to pieces, then, focus first on how your reader will benefit from what they are going to read. You'll have failed if your reader gets to the end of your article and thinks 'So what?' Keep in mind, always, that your first reader will be the editor you hope to sell the piece to. Your aim, every time, must be to inspire, encourage and enthuse first the editor and then the reader, so that they'll both be looking out for your next article—and eventually for your book.

### Make a note

- Successful how-to writers focus on their readers' reactions to what they write, not on showing off how much they know.

## The different article forms

Here are some of the most frequently used forms:

1. Problem-solving: telling one person's story, giving the readers information they can apply to a particular problem of their own.
2. Case history: most usual in health or psychology pieces. Such stories should be true, with only the names changed to avoid recognition. You might include several case histories, to look at a problem from different angles.
3. Advice from an expert—or perhaps a celebrity who has 'overcome shyness', 'lost five stones in weight', 'conquered an addiction' and the like, under an 'as told to' byline.
4. Anecdotal: brief stories told in sequence to illustrate a topic. Less formal than a case history, anecdotes can convey information on even the most sombre or complex subject in an easily digestible way. Include statistics, quotes from experts, and explanatory passages to link the stories.
5. Step-by-step: most usually associated with practical how-to writing, this format can work well in lifestyle pieces too, for example, 'Don't let shyness ruin the party—six easy steps to a fun night out'.
6. Round-up: a gathering of advice on the same topic from several different sources. For example, you might ask half a dozen young mothers about how they coped with the pleasures and problems of their child's first day at school.

## Writing a strong article

Whatever type of how-to article you want to sell, you need to make it as strong in structure and content and as easy to read as possible. Here's how to make your practical article a hit with your target editor:

- Keep sentences and paragraphs short. Keep instructions simple, clear and concise.
- Keep your introduction brief. For example: 'A home-made party cake gives your special occasion that personal touch. Here are six beauties to bake and decorate yourself.' Then go straight into the meat of the piece.
- List the required tools and/or ingredients right after the introduction. Advise the reader to gather all the materials together in one place before beginning the project, whether he's going to bake a cake or make a rock garden. He then has everything he needs to hand and in the right place, and won't have to leave the job, perhaps at a crucial stage, to go and look for a missing ingredient or a different tool. If the job requires an uncommon or hard-to-find piece of equipment, make this clear, and be sure to tell your reader where he can get hold of it and what it will cost. Vagueness irritates.
- Check and double-check all the measurements you give— they need to be as precise as possible. For example, in cake-making, specify exactly what you mean by a teaspoonful: is it level or heaped? By 'a cupful', do you mean a coffee cup, a tea cup, a breakfast cup, or bucket-sized? Avoid woolly instructions like 'Place in a medium-hot oven.' Medium-hot to one person's hand might be roasting-hot to another's. Specify the temperature. State exactly what size cake-tin is required and so on.
- Give all measurements in both imperial and metric figures. Younger people won't know a yard from an ounce, and older people could be flummoxed by millimetres and centimetres. Give temperatures in both Celsius and Fahrenheit. Don't require your readers to make complicated conversions.
- Use active voice, not passive or conditional voice. 'Separate the egg yolks from the whites and put the yolks in a mixing bowl' is sharper and more authoritative than 'The egg yolks should be separated from the whites and placed

in a mixing bowl.' The strong active voice reassures the reader that you, the writer, know your business.

- Wherever you can, give reasons for your instructions. People will understand more clearly and remember better if they know the reasons why a job should be done in a particular way. For example, in a piece on how to sew a zip fastener into a garment: 'Keep the zip fastener closed throughout the process. This will keep the fabric edges together, giving a much neater finish than you could achieve by sewing each side separately.'

- Use common technical terms where appropriate, but explain them as you go. Don't assume knowledge—your reader might be a complete novice.

- Use simple concise language: 'begin' not 'commence', 'now' not 'at this moment in time', 'most' not 'a great many of' and so on.

- Count the number of times 'I' appears against the frequency of 'you'. If there's too much emphasis on 'I', your article is likely to fail. It's 'you' and 'your' that will interest your reader. Faced with constant references to 'I', 'me', 'my', he'll wonder what's in it for him.

## Successful interviewing

Readers are always interested in other people's ways of doing things, especially if they are hearing from experts. Interviewing is a way to get both information and quotes to authenticate and liven up your article. Sometimes, indeed, an interview with an expert or with a person with an interesting story to tell can make a whole piece.

Interviews don't always have to be done in person. They can be done by phone or by e-mail; although face-to-face interviews offer more chance to pick up on body language, facial gestures, and spontaneous comments.

Here are a few tips on getting the best from your interview subject:

- For an in-person interview, dress appropriately. If you're meeting in a hotel or restaurant, observe the venue's dress code. If you're invited to your subject's home, 'smart casual' is usually suitable.

- When you're setting up the interview, agree the time-span both you and your subject are happy to give to the interview. Somewhere between forty-five minutes and an hour-and-a-half should be enough.

- Arrive on time. Carry a mobile phone with you so you can let your interviewee know if you're held up. Remember to switch off your phone during the interview.

- Don't start firing questions straight away. Take time to put your subject at ease, but don't bore him or her with too much personal chit-chat.

- For in-person interviews, you need to learn shorthand or some other form of speedwriting. You must be able to read your notes back—on the spot, if you're asked—and to transcribe them accurately later. (Interviewing by e-mail doesn't pose this problem—see below.) Always carry spare pens and notebook.

- For in-person interviews you also need a tape recorder, the more compact and discreet the better—an obtrusive piece of equipment could hamper relaxation. An on-the-spot recording could be vital if there's any query about what you write later. Make sure you have spare batteries and tapes. Always ask permission, though, before you use a recorder. Transcribe your recordings as soon as possible after the interview, while the conversation is still fresh in your memory. This is particularly important if your interviewee speaks quickly or has a heavy accent.

- Take a camera. Ask your subject if he or she is willing for you to take an informal shot or two. If it's a well-known person, they might provide you with a ready-made publicity photo.

- Never go into an interview unprepared. Read up on your interview subject as much as possible beforehand. If the answers to basic background questions are readily available in published articles, biographies and so on, you won't make a good impression if you let your interviewee see that you haven't done your homework.

- Have the focus of your interview clear in your mind, and prepare a list of written questions in advance. If the answers you're getting are not as clear, full or pertinent as you would like, ask additional questions till you're happy with the responses you have.
- Don't ask 'closed' questions, the kind that invite a 'Yes' or 'No' answer. Ask open-ended questions—remember our old friends Who, What, Where, When, Why, and How. For example, not 'Do you like the new soluble oil paints?' but 'What do you think of the new soluble oil paints?'
- For interviews by telephone, have a recording device to hand and ask your subject's permission to record the conversation. As with face-to-face interviews, always have your questions well prepared in advance.

### Interviewing by e-mail

While it's easy and convenient to do, you should be aware that e-interviewing is sometimes looked on with suspicion by editors. The writer has no way of checking that an interviewee's responses have not been influenced by other interested parties like publicists wishing to push a particular angle (or even a product).

Sometimes, though, this is the only way you'll be able to interview a particularly elusive subject—just don't take everything they tell you at face value.

E-interviewing can work well if you already know the interviewee—perhaps you've met them socially or at a conference, and are confident they'll deal honourably with you.

Think your questions out carefully, base them on well researched background knowledge, and put them in a logical order. Your subject will then—you hope—reply in likewise logical fashion. It's easy, too, to ask for clarification of any reply you don't clearly understand. This is a great time-saver.

E-interviews can be useful, too, if you're writing a round-up article, gathering opinions, tips and so on from a number of people.

Don't forget to acknowledge the replies and say 'Thank you'. The informality of e-mail can sometimes encourage over-casual attitudes.

The downside of e-interviewing is that it's all too easy for your material to be copied on to other parties without your knowledge, maybe by a subject who wants other people's opinions on what he should say to you. So if you're working on something you want to keep exclusive, e-mail is probably not the best way.

## Writing and submitting seasonal material

The term 'seasonal material' refers to writing related to a particular season of the year. Christmas, New Year, Easter, Mother's Day, Father's Day, Hallowe'en, Guy Fawkes Night and so on offer a wealth of opportunities for the how-to writer.

Seasonal material aimed at magazines must be submitted well ahead of the occasion. Lead times vary, but you need to work at least six months in advance, possibly even as long as a year ahead for monthly publications. Check your target magazine's seasonal deadlines.

As I write this section, it's early March and the weekend papers and supplements are packed with articles, short and long, on spring-cleaning. From 'How to spring-clean your make-up bag' to 'Spring-clean your love-life', readers are urged to blow away the cobwebs and make a fresh start.

Magazines, too, are packed with spring features. Most of these pieces will have been in the pipeline since well before Christmas. They certainly won't have come from anything that arrived on an editor's desk last month. Submit your seasonal offerings in plenty of time.

It's a good idea, in fact, to write seasonal material during the relevant season, ready to submit in time for next year. It makes sense, doesn't it, to write your Christmas how-to pieces while the season is still all around you and you're alert to what needs to be done and what problems need to be dealt with. It's hard to get that 'Jingle Bells' feeling when you're sitting on a beach with the sun scorching the keys of your laptop.

*Make a note*

- Try not to tie your seasonal offerings to a particular year. If an editor likes what you offer, but has already filled her allocated space for that year, she might want to hold your work over for next year's season. If your piece is focused on a specific year, she can't do this.
- It makes sense to write seasonal material during the season, for submission the following year.

## Dealing with illustrations

If you want to sell practical how-to pieces, you'll almost certainly be expected to supply illustrative material. Most magazines nowadays prefer digital images, but you should check this, in the guidelines, on the website, or direct with the editorial office.

Some of the 'quality' magazines insist on professional standard large format photos, which you might not be able to produce. However, these superior quality photographs are mainly used for magazine covers, with digital images used on the inside pages. If you plan to make photographs a major feature in your writing career, it will pay you to take a course at college or evening classes. Not everyone has a natural eye for a good picture.

*Make a note*

- Check with the magazine what kind of photographs they prefer. Find the information in their guidelines, on the website, or phone the office and ask.

Think about commercial companies, too. They'll often be happy to supply professional photographs to illustrate your piece if it's likely to generate good publicity for their products. For an article on, say, cultivating dahlias, a nursery or a garden centre might be pleased to supply professional photos if you can guarantee the company prominent attribution as the source.

If your piece requires instructional diagrams, you don't need to be an artist to do these. Simply sketch your diagrams as clearly as you can, indicating measurements, proportions and so on, and the magazine will commission an artist to turn your sketches into professional illustrations.

For self-help and art-of-living pieces, most publications keep a stock of photographs posed by models, from which they'll choose something appropriate. It's possible, though, that if your article is centred on personal experience, either of yourself, your family, or someone you've interviewed, the magazine might make acceptance conditional on you or your subject being willing either to supply photos or to be photographed by a staff photographer. Personal experience pieces published in reputable magazines are almost invariably genuine, although the names might be changed in the printed piece.

### Make a note

● Good illustrations will increase your chances of selling your article.

## Keeping records of your sources

Suppose you are writing an article on how to cope with a child who has a chronic illness. You might want to back up your advice with statistics about the frequency of that particular condition in the population, what medical advances have been and are being made and so on, and perhaps supplementing your piece with a sidebar giving sources of further information and advice. You need to keep a record of where you found any statistics and other facts you give, sources of quotations and so on. Some publications require you to supply a note of your sources when you submit your article, others might ask you later to supply details, especially if they receive requests from readers wanting to check the authenticity of what you have told them.

Or perhaps you want to write about how to choose the most suitable holiday destination for a young family. Be sure to keep detailed notes on where you got your information, who advised you for or against specific places and so on.

## Why you shouldn't write the article yet

You don't want to spend time, do you, writing hundreds, maybe thousands of words you might have to rewrite in a different style for a different publication, or even fail to sell at all?

Go about the job in a professional way by approaching your target publication's editor with a query letter, as you'll be shown in Chapter 6. Don't write the whole article until an editor expresses an interest in what you're offering. You can gather material, check facts, write an outline, do any kind of preparation you feel will help you be ready to write the piece quickly, but don't actually write it till an editor asks to see it. Your time is valuable. Don't put yourself in a position where you might have to write the article more than once.

The only exception to this general marketing rule is humour. No editor can assess a humorous piece on the strength of a query.

## Widen your market options with lateral thinking

By thinking laterally and using your imagination, you can widen your market options considerably. Here's an example you could adapt to suit your own interests: An article on how to take successful photographs appeared as the lead feature in a specialist car magazine. Why? Because every photograph—and they were superb—showed a different model of the marque to which the magazine was devoted.

The same article could have featured in a top-class photography magazine. That's an example not only of imaginative thinking but also of hedging your bets!

## Is it really writer's block?

If you get stuck—and we all run out of steam sometimes— please don't elevate this temporary hiccup to the status of writer's block.

I'm not saying that writer's block doesn't exist. It does happen. If you're physically ill, or have suffered some kind of emotional trauma, your brain blocks out everything that isn't essential to your physical and mental survival. It happens, too, when a writer has just completed a major project and has 'written themselves dry'. The brain simply says 'Enough for now.'

This is not the same condition as finding it hard to get started in the morning, looking for other things that desperately need doing, suddenly craving another cup of coffee … anything to avoid that blank page.

Consider this: Have you ever heard of a case of bus-driver's block? Nurse's block? Signalman's block?

You're not writing the Great British Novel here. You're dealing with the practicalities of life, with solid facts, not with flights of the creative imagination.

Real writers write. They apply the seat of the pants to the seat of the chair and they write. That's what they do. If you're serious about your writing, that is what you must do, too, however hard it might seem.

Norah Ephron put it this way: 'I'm a journalist. If I get writer's block I get fired!'

## Points to remember

- Any competent writer can write how-to articles.
- You need never run out of ideas for how-to writing.
- It's essential to focus on how your article will benefit the reader.
- The 'why' is just as important as the 'how' in how-to writing.
- Give careful thought to the best form for your how-to article.
- Submit seasonal material well before the season.

# 6 Approaching your market

## Newspapers and magazines—the differences in approach

You can write how-to material for both newspapers and magazines. Both media offer the same challenges to the freelance writer: the need for detailed study of their content and style, and a professional approach to selling your material.

The main difference for the writer lies in the lead times. You can write up a piece for a newspaper and see it in print the following day, whereas even the most frequently published magazines, the weeklies, have lead times of at least a few weeks.

Because of their frequency and their methods of production, newspapers use up material faster than magazines do. Most editors are willing to look at appropriate material from freelances who approach them in a business-like way.

## Writing for your local paper

If you're just starting out, try your local paper. You probably know the publication well, and you might even know people on the staff, but you should still approach the editor as professional to professional.

By their nature, local papers focus mainly on local news and local events. (You might recall the often-told story of the headline 'High Street Grocer Lost at Sea' over a report on the sinking of the Titanic.)

Any how-to material you offer them should also have some local interest. In a piece on, for example, how to choose the best spring bedding plants, you might gather advice from local gardeners and park keepers. Before you offer anything, though, you would be wise to check that the paper doesn't already have a regular gardening contributor. You'll get a fast refusal if you tread on someone else's turf.

Another way to break in is to interview local people who have done something out of the ordinary. Perhaps you know someone who has set up a local craft group or opened their garden to the public for charity. Writing the interview up as a 'They did it, so can you' type of how-to could work well and get your foot in the door.

### Make a note

- Local papers focus closely on local people and events only.

## Writing for regional papers

Newspapers that cover a wider regional area are not so different from local papers, in that they focus on the interests of a readership that is limited in geographical scope. The same caveats apply: look for gaps in the coverage rather than trying to compete with an established writer.

Again, human interest pieces with a how-to angle are always welcome.

# Writing for national papers

The big dailies and weekend papers have a voracious appetite for material. Look at all those supplements that, for example, *The Guardian* produces every week: Education, Film & Music, Media, Office Hours, Society, Technology and more. The *Guardian*'s entry in the *Writers' & Artists' Yearbook* states, 'Few articles are taken from outside contributors except on its feature and specialist pages.' This tells you that you should concentrate on those pages rather than try to break into other parts of the paper.

*The Independent*'s supplements include: Business Review, Education, The Information, Media Weekly, Property Supplement, Review, Save & Spend, Traveller … Its *Yearbook* entry reads 'Occasional freelance contributions; preliminary letter advisable.'

And *The Daily Telegraph* supplements include: Arts & Books, Business 2 & Jobs, Gardening, Motoring, Property, Sport, Travel, and Your Money. In the *Yearbook*, they say, 'Articles on a wide range of subjects of topical interest considered. Preliminary letter and synopsis required.'

Always follow submission advice when it's given; this will show you've done your homework.

### Make a note

- Follow any advice on submission methods offered by a publication. Writers who disregard such advice brand themselves either as amateurs or as rebels. Editors have little time for either.

Are you reaching for a pen already? Supplements like these are hungry for how-to material. Their readers are looking for sound advice and insider know-how on every kind of subject. They can never get enough. And payment is high. As a first-timer you might not be able to command National Union of Journalists rates (see *The Writer's Handbook* for current rates), but you'll be well rewarded nonetheless.

Here are a few tips on writing for newspapers:

- Offer only material you're sure will interest the readership.
- Offer only material written in the newspaper's specific style. Some papers publish style guides on their website or in print, but you should be able to work out the style you should write in by studying recent issues in detail.
- Offer only material that complies with the paper's stated length limits (see their guidelines or the yearbooks).
- Offer only material written to the absolute best of your ability—don't rely on someone else editing the piece for you. Unless you're someone whose name will draw readers, they won't want to be bothered.
- Keep letters of enquiry as concise and sharp as possible— and write them in the newspaper's style.
- When you agree to a deadline for delivery of material, make sure you keep it. If you get a reputation for being unreliable, you'll quickly be dropped.
- Remember that newspaper editors work under intense pressure. If you keep sending them unsuitable material or otherwise waste their time, they'll soon tell you to get lost.
- When you're starting out, don't argue about the amount of money you're offered. That doesn't mean you should write for nothing, but until you've proved your worth to the publication, accept the editor's valuation. Once you're established, you'll be in a stronger position to argue for higher fees.

### Make a note

- Newspaper editors work under extreme pressure. The wise writer keeps his demands on the editor's time and patience to a minimum.

In Chapter 3 we looked in detail at writing for magazines. Much of what you've just read about writing for newspapers applies to magazines, too. To recap:

- Be professional in everything you do.
- Offer only material that's 100 per cent suitable for your target market.

- Tailor your offering carefully to that market.
- Remember to take account of your market's lead times.

# Writing an article query

If your article is very short—less than 700 words or so—send the complete manuscript. The editor would have to spend as long reading your query as it would take to read the piece.

The only other exception to the query rule is humour. As you read in Chapter 5, you can't explain humour. Either you can write humour or you can't. You'll seldom get a firm acceptance for humour on the strength of a query anyway, so you might as well show the editor how good you are.

For any other kind of how-to article, whether you want to offer it to a newspaper or to a magazine, you need to pitch the idea in a query letter. Don't be scared by this. It's to your benefit that you won't slog for hours, maybe days, writing an article for a particular market and then find you have to rewrite it for a different market altogether.

Make your query as interesting and concise as you can. Use bullet points to summarise the content. This method will allow the editor to see what you're offering without having to read through long discursive paragraphs. Your query should show the editor:

1. Your topic, and the angle you plan to take on it.
2. How the reader will benefit from what you tell them.
3. Your *relevant* qualifications for writing the piece—personal experience, academic credits, awards gained, prizes won…

### Make a note

- You'll impress the editor by making your query concise and easy to digest.

### An example of how to write a query

Here's an idea that could interest a parenting magazine, a women's magazine, a building society magazine, or possibly a newspaper supplement. It comes from my own experience of moving home from one city to another with a school-age child,

Molly Keene   5 Penman Way   Writersville   XX5 5XX
Tel: 01011 110111 E-mail: MollyK@ISP.co.uk

28th October 20XX

John Selector
Editor
Great Mums and Dads Magazine
6 Nursery Slopes
Toytown MX1 1MX

Dear Mr Selector

Imagine a family arriving in a strange city, knowing no one, with a young daughter who has had to leave her friends behind and is faced with starting at a new school.

This happened to us, but we were helped enormously by our new neighbours who introduced us to the local 'vacation club'. This club had been formed by local parents to keep the children occupied and off the streets during school holidays. It was an absolute boon to us, and I feel sure that parents and children in other districts would benefit greatly if more such clubs could be set up.

I would like to offer you an article on this topic, which I believe would interest your readers. The article would cover:

- The benefits such a scheme brings to the whole community.
- How to contact like-minded people—word of mouth and editorial coverage in the local paper work best; once the club is up and running, a regular notice in the 'local events' column of the paper alerts newcomers to its existence.
- How to set up the club—a committee of parents makes all the decisions.
- How to finance the enterprise—mainly through fund-raising events, with the possibility of council grants once the club is up and running successfully.
- How to decide what activities would interest the children—we have a huge range, from chess tournaments in winter to trips to the coast in summer, from craft groups to carefully supervised

visits to factories and other commercial enterprises; there is always something to suit all ages and abilities.

- Who would organise and run events—individual parents or groups of parents contribute their skills and special interests, and hire premises, arrange insurance etc if the events are too big to run in private homes.
- Summary of benefits.

I have been active in running our vacation club for four years now, and feel able to write about the project with authority and enthusiasm.

The wordage would be to comply with your requirements, offered at your usual rates. I could supply photographs taken at some of the events (with the parents' permission, of course).

I enclose a stamped addressed envelope, and look forward to hearing from you in due course. Thank you.

Yours sincerely
Molly Keene.

**Figure 2. Example of a query letter.**

and knowing no one when we arrived in our new location. We found it easy to settle in because we soon discovered a long-established 'vacation club', run by local parents for children aged between ten and sixteen. This is a topic that should interest a wide range of readers now that more and more people are relocating for business, domestic and economic reasons. (You're welcome to use the idea if it appeals to you!)

Figure 2 on page 82–3 shows how to construct a query on this topic.

## E-queries

We live in a fast-moving digital age, and many editors now prefer an initial approach by e-mail. This can be wonderfully time-saving; negotiations that used to take weeks by snail-mail can now be done in just a few hours.

Such ease and speed, however, can be hazardous for the unwary writer. Handled inappropriately, your e-mail query could alienate your target editor before he reads a word of it. The following tips will help you write e-mail queries that sell.

## Electronic etiquette

1. First of all, check that your target market accepts approaches by e-mail. You'll be wasting your time sending an e-mail query, however brilliant, to a market that doesn't want it. It will simply be deleted without being read. If you can't find this information in the guidelines, on the website, or in the writers' market handbooks, call the editorial office and ask.

   If it's okay to e-mail, check whether they want your query pasted into the body of the e-mail or sent as an attachment. Many publications refuse attachments because of the danger of viruses. Check the required format for file attachments.

2. Keep it simple. Don't use fancy fonts or colourful letterheads, and don't include graphics—all these take up unnecessary bandwidth space and can be slow to download.

3. Keep it short. One single-spaced page, two at most, should be enough.

4. Be sure the idea you're offering is strong, well thought out, and appropriate to your target market. The purpose of your query is to persuade the editor that your idea is a brilliant one that will delight her readers, and that you are the ideal person to write the piece. Always keep in mind that the editor is looking to fill each issue with material so good and so right for her readers that they will rush out to buy her next issue—and the next and the next...

5. Don't be too casual. E-mail tends to encourage informality. Resist this. Adopt a conventional and formal tone. Don't use first names on first contact. As you build a good relationship with the editor, you'll probably get on to first-name terms quite soon, but avoid over-familiarity at this early stage. You certainly won't make a

favourable first impression if you open with 'Hi, Millie!' or 'Hello, Bill!' And you know by now, don't you, how vital it is to address your query to a person by name, never 'Dear Editor' or 'To whom it may concern'.

6. Use the subject line to your advantage. Avoid anything that might be mistaken for spam. Start the subject line with the word 'Query'. 'Query: Ten Ways to Cut your Household Bills' will be read. A subject line that says 'Free yourself from household debt' will be deleted. Internet Service Providers are policing e-mail with ever-increasing vigilance, are constantly reviewing their spam alerts, and will block any e-mail whose subject line contains words on their current 'no-no' list. For example, don't use 'free', 'offer', 'bargain', 'one-off' and the like.

7. Be sure to give your complete contact information. As well as your e-mail address, include your full postal address, home and mobile telephone numbers, and your fax number if you have one. Make it as easy as possible for the editor to contact you.

8. Spell-check your query. Then print it out and read it on paper. You won't impress the editor if you send a query that has typos, misspellings or errors of punctuation or syntax. Use your query to convince the editor that you're a first-class writer who can be trusted to supply work that's impeccable in every way. See page 151 for tips on proof-reading.

9. If you can supply samples of published work, offer to send them but don't include them with your query. If you're not already published, say nothing! If you have a website where you can display your samples, mention this, but don't expect a busy editor to go there.

10. Don't shoot off simultaneous queries to several magazines. E-mail almost invites this practice by making it easy to do, but editors develop a nose for a query that's even a shade too general. If they suspect that the same piece might be on offer to rival publications they might not bother to reply.

11. Allow the editor time to consider your query with the care it deserves. If the guidelines give a response time, respect this. If you've heard nothing beyond that

response time, send a polite e-mail enquiring about the status of your query, giving the subject heading and the date you sent it. Be discreet, though—editors are busy people, and the delete button is only a fingertip away.

12. It's a good idea to save all your queries in a file, whether they've been successful or not. You might find other openings where you can use them in the future.

### Make a note

- Craft your e-query with the care you would give to any other query letter.

## Writing 'on spec'

When you're starting out as a freelance, you'll be expected to write a fair amount of material 'on spec'. That means you'll have to be prepared to do quite a lot of work speculatively, with no guarantee the editor will accept anything, even if she has asked to see it.

Even established writers have to do this at times, perhaps to get a foothold in a new publication, or to break into an established market they've never written for before.

Don't feel resentful about this. After all, the editor's reputation is on the line, and possibly the future viability of her magazine. No editor can afford to give a guarantee of acceptance to a writer she hasn't worked with before, even on the strength of an irresistible query. You need to prove you can deliver what you've promised—every time and on time.

As you establish your reputation as a writer who can be relied on not only to deliver copy that lives up to your query but to deliver it to deadline, you'll find yourself being asked more and more to write on commission rather than 'on spec'. So be patient, and keep at it. The only writer who is sure to fail is the writer who gives up.

### Make a note

- Don't forget to keep a careful note of your submissions, as outlined in Chapter 3.

While you're waiting for a response…

Get all your material together. Check that you have everything you need, so that you can write and submit your article quickly when an editor invites you to send it.

You've already studied your target market's style, you have your article outline from which you wrote your query, so you should be all set to go.

Once you've sent the finished piece off, don't sit back and wait. There's no guarantee you'll get an acceptance, so get on with developing other ideas, other projects. The more queries you send out, the higher your chances of success.

You don't need to confine your efforts to this country, either…

## Writing for overseas magazines

There's a great big English-speaking world out there. The *Writers' & Artists' Yearbook* lists magazines in Australia, New Zealand, South Africa, Canada and the United States of America. A search on the internet will also show potential markets for English-language material in other countries where English is widely known, like India. And don't forget all those ex-pats living in Europe. Many ex-pat communities have their own English-language magazines. As well as offering new work to these markets, you can also sell material you've already published in the UK—*provided you've only sold British rights in that material.*

The biggest market by far is the USA. The best source of information about American markets is the annual *Writer's Market*, which is like a super-size *Yearbook*. *Writer's Market* is published by Writer's Digest Books, publishers of *Writer's Digest* magazine. Some larger branches of Waterstone's stock *Writer's Market*, or they can order it for you. Some branches also stock copies of *Writer's Digest* magazine. *Writer's Digest* has an excellent website (www.writersdigest.com) where you can read features from the magazine, check out new markets, and sign up to receive a regular free e-mail newsletter with features and market news.

A UK version of *Writer's Market* has been launched by publishers David & Charles, a rival to the established British guides. Don't confuse this with the American guide.

Most American magazines provide comprehensive guidelines as standard practice, either on their websites or by post in return for a stamped addressed envelope, or one sent with International Reply Coupons (IRCs), making life much simpler for the writer and saving editors precious time. Following the guidelines will improve your chances of success. Some of the websites also offer online copies of the magazine so you can easily do an in-depth market study.

When you send work abroad, remember to enclose a big enough self-addressed envelope plus enough IRCs for the return of your work. If your manuscript is disposable, say so—but you still need to enclose a business-size envelope plus two IRCs for their reply. If you have an e-mail address, include that in your covering letter. If you prefer, you can buy US postage stamps online at www.usps.com, the website of the United States Postal Service, where you can also find current postage rates and other information about the service.

Invest in an American-English dictionary. Many spellings—and also some meanings—are different from the English language as we speak it in the UK. You'll impress the editor if you can write like a pro, in 'American' English.

If rights required are not specified, offer 'First North American Rights'. These rights also cover Canada, so don't submit the same material to both American and Canadian magazines.

### Make a note

- Go on—be adventurous. Search out an overseas market and go for it.

## Commissions and kill fees

Once you've proved your value and reliability, and begun to make a name for yourself, you could find your queries being answered with a firm commission to write your article. You might even find editors offering you topics they want you to write about. This means that your article will be published unless unforeseen circumstances prevent this, like a new editor sweeping with a ruthless broom or the publication folding.

In the latter event, you have to accept that you've had bad luck, and try to place your work elsewhere. However, if the publication decides not to use work that you've been commissioned to write and that you've delivered on time and to standard, you should be entitled to a kill fee, a percentage of the agreed payment.

You can see, then, that it's vital to have the agreement in writing, showing the terms under which the piece was commissioned. If the commission was made and the terms agreed in writing, either by post or by e-mail, there should be no problem, but if you were called on the telephone, write a letter or send an e-mail to the commissioning editor the same day, detailing the agreement—and keep a copy. You might need to produce this as evidence that you're entitled to your kill fee.

### Make a note

- If you're commissioned via a telephone call, always confirm the terms agreed by letter or by e-mail the same day, and keep a copy.

## Points to remember

- Local papers only want local-interest material.
- National newspaper supplements offer opportunities for how-to writing.
- Take time to create an interesting query letter for a magazine article—but don't write the complete piece till you have an editor's interest.
- Craft e-mail queries with caution.
- Be prepared to write 'on spec'.
- Try writing for overseas markets—there are plenty to choose from.
- Always get the details of a commission on paper.

# 7 **Writing the article**

Picture the scene: The letter you've been hoping for has arrived. Your query has hit the target and the editor wants to see your article. All you have to do is write it!

Now you need to check that you've selected the most appropriate form and style for the magazine's readership. If you get the whole picture wrong, you'll disappoint both the editor and yourself. The example in Figure 3 shows an example of structure and style appropriate to one article.

## Structure

Please read the article printed in Figure 3. It's a short how-to article of mine, published in *Freelance Writing & Photography Magazine*. (This long-established writers' magazine

### Word Processing? Believe me, you'll love it!

By Chriss McCallum

**'Technophobe: A person who fears and dislikes technology' (The Chambers Dictionary, 1993 edition).**

Is this you?

During a course I led regularly, I touched on word processing. The very mention raised groans and murmurs of 'Don't understand computers', 'My trusty Olivetti will see me out' and so on. There is still a lot of resistance around, especially among older writers. Yet I haven't come across a single one who regrets moving on from the traditional typewriter.

Word processing programs come as standard in personal computers nowadays. However technical it sounds, word processing is not a high technology skill. Once you've got the hang of how the 'processing' works, you'll never look back. Believe me. If I can do it, so can you. (I still have problems setting the video recorder.)

The first thing you learn in word processing is: Don't press the return key at the end of the line. You only use the return key to begin a new paragraph or to insert a line space. Why? In a word, word-wrapping.

The word processor automatically runs (wraps) the text over on to the next line as you type. Think of your text as a stream of words flowing unbroken through a paragraph. This means that whatever alterations you make within that paragraph, your continuous stream of text absorbs them into the flow and moves the text forward or back to accommodate the changes. You can delete or insert characters, words, even whole sentences, and the text adapts itself seamlessly with no further effort from you.

Isn't that a boon? No more retyping a whole page because you've made an error that can't be 'invisibly mended'. No more retyping a whole chapter because you've added or taken out a few lines on the first page.

Magic? That's only the beginning.

Look at some of the labour- and time-saving facilities word processing offers. You can:

- Store your work in an electronic memory, and recall any part of your writing to the screen to work on as and when you choose.
- Correct, delete, insert any amount of material on-screen.
- Move text around, transposing characters, words, sentences, para-graphs, pages, whole chapters if you like, by 'cutting' and 'pasting' on-screen.
- Change any specified word throughout the text using the 'search and replace' facility. (Suppose you've typed 70,000 words of your novel when you decide it was a mistake to call your heroine 'Amaryllis'. 'Daisy' would suit her better. Imagine the work and the time it would take if you had to change every 'Amaryllis' to 'Daisy' one by one!)
- Have an inbuilt thesaurus literally at your fingertips.
- Along with an inbuilt spellchecker if you need one.
- Have an automatic word counter.
- Number your pages automatically.
- Polish your work to a fine finish before you print it out, thus pro-ducing a crisp, clean, error-free professional-looking manuscript.
- Store or send your work in an electronic file as well as on paper.

Most publishers still require a print-out as well as a disk. You need a decent printer to produce a clear, easily readable, script. Editors pre-fer a plain roman serif typeface. Readability is the key.

If you're serious about developing a writing career, a computer with a word processing program and a disk drive is essential. With any of the recognised market leaders, you'll be able to upgrade and add-on for years to come.

I quote from the American *Writer's Market*: 'Many publishers are accepting or even requesting that final manuscript submissions be made on computer disk. This saves the magazine or book publisher the expense of having your manuscript typeset, and can be helpful in the editing stage. The publisher will simply download your fin-ished manuscript into the computer system they use to produce their product.'

The UK is already following the US lead. Don't get left behind.

One caveat to potential technophiles: as you get to know and love your word processor, you'll have to resist its only danger. It's so easy to use, it can trigger that insidious affliction, wordiness. But that's another story.

**Figure 3. Example of a published how-to article.**

fell victim to an unsympathetic change of ownership—see 'Don't get complacent', on page 108.)

I offered this article in a query letter that included a one-sentence overview and an outline, with a suggested length of 1,000 words. The editor liked the idea, but asked me to write the piece to a maximum of 700 words, due to space restrictions in the issue in which he wanted to use it. To fit into this limited wordage, the article had to be written with strict economy. As it was aimed at older writers, whose concerns about the new technology ranged from slight apprehension to extreme nervousness, its tone had to be warm and encouraging. It's worth looking at a brief analysis of how this was done.

- The opening: Using the dictionary quotation set in bold as a standfirst is designed to catch the reader's attention. The three-word question 'Is this you?' standing alone as the first paragraph after the quotation makes it clear which readers are being addressed.
- Paragraph 2 states the problem with a mild touch of humour, but not unkindly.
- Paragraph 3 reassures the readers that they will be able to deal with the problem.
- Paragraphs 4 and 5 explain how word processing works for the writer. They are written in a non-technical way, with the only slightly technical term (word-wrapping) clearly explained.
- The next dozen paragraphs explain to the readers exactly how word processing will help them, with the list of benefits laid out in separate bullet-pointed sections for clarity.
- Paragraph 19 moves on to more general comments on the need to use word processing in today's writing business.

- Paragraphs 20, 21 and 22 look to the way the industry is turning more and more to electronic submissions.
- And the final paragraph rounds the piece off with a light-hearted warning about the technology's tendency to encourage over-writing.

This example shows how a straightforward uncomplicated structure works best when you're explaining how to solve a problem to people who instinctively want to put off dealing with it. The simple point-by-point layout encourages confidence, as does the reassuring and informal tone.

### Make a note

- Keep the structure of your article as simple and straightforward as you can.
- Make sure the paragraphs flow logically one into another, with no jarring breaks.

## Style

The best advice I can offer you about style in writing how-to material is to write as if you were explaining your topic in a letter to a friend—as though you're talking on paper.

Don't make the mistake of striving for a distinctive style. Trying too hard can lead to a stilted, artificial tone that intrudes between the reader and the text. Develop your own voice, certainly, but try to keep it natural and, above all, avoid pretentious language. Write to express, not to impress. Don't be tempted to reach for the thesaurus every five minutes. Your aim is to make your writing as clear as you possibly can, so that what you want to say does not get obscured by the way in which you say it. Aim for a conversational tone, and avoid 'writerly' prose.

That said, you also need to meld your own natural style with the style of the publication or publishing house you're writing for. Many an otherwise interesting and well-written piece has winged its way home because the writer hasn't bothered either to research or to follow the required house style.

In general, though, keep it simple and keep it tight. Your reader wants advice and information, not a literary masterpiece.

I would like you to look at several different types of how-to article in magazines and newspapers. Study them for form and style. Ask yourself why they work. If you think they could be better, ask yourself 'How?'

Get into the habit of looking at how-to articles with an analytical eye. This will help you develop your critical instincts when you're revising your own how-to writing.

## Getting rid of the flab

Cut 'wordiness' out of your writing. Don't use five words where one will do. This is especially necessary in articles, where you'll have to fit everything you want to say into a specified and tightly limited number of words. Here are a few of the phrases that commonly show up in wordy writing:

| Wordy | Neat |
|---|---|
| at this moment in time | now |
| a great many of | most |
| in the event that | if |
| with the result that | so/thus/therefore |
| in order to | to |

Check your writing for redundant words. We all have favourites that can creep in quietly while we're not looking. My own weakness is 'very'. Other writers I know have to check their work for too-frequent use of common words like 'that' or 'just' or 'quite' or 'pretty'.

Try, too, to clear your writing of words and phrases you see in print all too often. Avoid clichéd phrases like:

'bold as brass'
'like the plague'
'a level playing field'
'the writing's on the wall'
'as quick as a flash'

'back to square one'
'at the drop of a hat'
'the tip of the iceberg'…

## Standfirsts

Look at the articles in any magazines you have to hand. Most will have a supplementary sentence or two after the heading, rather like an expanded sub-heading. The opening of the article shown in Figure 3 is an example of a standfirst. Here are a couple of other examples.

- From *Psychologies* magazine (February 2007 issue): Title: 'I'm short-tempered'. Standfirst: 'Does your anger get you—and your blood pressure—into trouble? Learn to control it, says Catherine Jones'.
- From *The Artist* magazine (February 2007 issue): title: 'Surprisingly versatile egg tempera'. Standfirst: 'Tempera is normally perceived as a demanding medium, but Mary Anne Aytoun-Ellis finds it ideal for both her small paintings and large-scale work'.

For practice, try writing your own versions of some of the standfirsts in the magazines you read. Then practise writing the standfirst you would like to see at the beginning of the article you're working on at the moment. Include the best version under the title when you're eventually ready to submit your query to an editor—your ability to write your own effective standfirst is a useful marketing tool and could help to sway the editor's decision in your favour.

## Sidebars

'Sidebar' is a publishing term describing a box set alongside the text, containing either additional information to supplement an article, or a restatement, for emphasis, of material already in the text. Sidebars can carry anything you feel you should include but that doesn't fit smoothly into your text, like reference material, definitions, contact addresses and so on.

Sidebars also serve the useful purpose of breaking up the page so that it looks more inviting to read than dense lines of text.

## Standard manuscript layout

Magazine editors and book publishers expect writers to submit material laid out in the standard manuscript format. Sloppy presentation could destroy your chances before anyone reads a word of what you've written.

Most publishing houses and magazine offices now operate with minimum staff. Long gone are the days when editors would persevere through an unprofessional-looking manuscript in the hope of discovering genius. They simply don't have the time. First impressions are vital—they separate the amateurs from the professionals. Don't let yourself down with substandard presentation.

Here's how to do it—see the example in Figure 4 on pages 100–101:

- All work must be typewritten or printed out from a computer or word processor.
- Use only plain white A4 paper of good quality and reasonable weight—80 gsm works well, as it's not too heavy but is strong enough to take a fair amount of handling and marking.
- Use a simple plain typeface, like Arial or Times New Roman in 12 point type size. Avoid any kind of non-standard typeface like italic, small capitals, condensed type and the like. Keep it simple—editors dislike anything that strains their eyes—understandable when you think of the amount of reading they have to do.
- Use black ink only, and make sure your print-out is clear and dark. Faint dregs-of-the-ink or last-legs-of-the-ribbon print won't be appreciated, and might not be read at all.
- Never send out anything printed in 'draft' mode.
- Set your typescript page to a standard format: margins of 50 mm (two inches) or so at the left and at least 25 mm (one inch) at the right. Editors and typographers need these

generous margins to mark corrections and instructions to the printer.

- Use double spacing, *not* single- or one-and-a-half-line spacing. Do not insert extra line spacing between paragraphs unless you want to indicate a line break in the text, in which case do not indent the first line of the paragraph after the line break.
- Have a uniform number of lines on each page except the first, where you have your title and byline at the beginning, and the last if your text ends short of the foot of the page.
- At the top right of the second and all following pages, insert a header identifying yourself as the author, the title of the article or book (abbreviated if necessary) and the page number. Leave at least one double space between the header and the text on each page.
- Number the pages in sequence throughout, from 'Page 1' to the end; for a book ms, do not number each chapter separately.
- Do not justify (make even) your text at the right-hand edge. Right-justification inserts extra spacing between words and complicates the printing.
- When you get to the end, type the word 'Ends' to indicate that the manuscript is complete.

### Make a note

- Learn to touch type. You're a professional writer with a lot of quality typing to do, and you don't have time to 'hunt and peck' around your keyboard. Take a course, or at least invest in a good typing manual like *Touch Typing in Ten Hours* by Ann Dobson.

## Revision and self-editing

Do try to finish your article well in advance of your deadline, to give yourself plenty of time to revise—and if necessary, rewrite—your piece. The time spent on that final checking

Fundraising is fun—Do it outdoors!

Flag days, fetes, festivals, fun-runs, fairs … the scope for outdoor fund-raising is as wide as your imagination and enterprise. Whatever your event, meticulous planning and detailed preparation are the keys to success, says Chriss McCallum.

Here are some ideas for outdoor events:

A street collection

The amount you raise from your street collection/flag day will be in direct proportion to the number of people out there collecting on your behalf, so you need to rally as many collectors as you possibly can. Don't expect any collector to do more than two hours at a stretch, especially in bad weather. (There will always be a few stalwarts who will insist on doing longer, but don't let them bully other people into thinking they must do the same.)

Inform the police that you have the necessary permit—they need to know that your collectors only, and no others, have permission to be out collecting that day.

Issue every collector with a badge and an identifying certificate, both of which should carry the collector's name and be signed by the organiser. Tins or boxes must be sealed and numbered, and you should keep a record of which collector takes out which number tin(s).

Etiquette

Make sure all your collectors understand the legal obligations and the etiquette of collecting in public places. They must not ask for money or block people's path or  shake tins in people's faces or behave in any way that could be held to be intimidating.

**Figure 4: Example of standard manuscript layout.**

and polishing can make the difference between acceptance and rejection. Remember that most publications run on a minimum of staff, and no one has time to spare to bring a roughly finished piece of work up to publication standard. That is your job.

If you build a reputation for submitting work that is accurate in every way, written in the required house style, to the right length, and ready to run, you'll quickly become the kind of valued contributor the editor can trust with regular commissions. Think how it will make you feel, to be the writer the editor calls with an offer of work, rather than the outsider trying to break in. It does happen, and it could happen to you.

So give yourself a decent breathing space—at least a day or two, if you can—between finishing the piece and checking it for faults. Here are the points to check and how to check them:

1. Have you organised your information in a way that will make sense to your readers?
2. Have you kept the focus of the piece on the core subject? Typically, you'll have gathered more information than you need to use, so it's important to leave out anything that might blur your meaning or lead your reader up an irrelevant byway.
3. Do your paragraphs follow on in a logical way, with smooth transitions one to the next? Are they in the right order for clarity of meaning?
4. Have you made your point or stated your argument so that your meaning is clear to your reader?
5. Have you used specific concrete terms, avoiding anything abstract?
6. Have you explained any technical or topic-specific terms clearly? An occasional touch of jargon, clarified and well defined, can lend authenticity.
7. Have you made the best use of paragraphing, section breaks and/or bullet points to help your reader follow your thinking?

8. Will your conclusion satisfy you reader? Have you tied up all the points you made? Have you delivered what you promised in your opening paragraph?

9. Is the tone and style of your writing appropriate for your readership?

10. Does your writing flow smoothly, so that your reader won't be distracted from your meaning by any inconsistency or awkwardness in the way you are saying it? Read your work aloud, if possible into a tape recorder. When you read aloud you can feel the rhythm and hear the cadence of your words. It's the best way to pick up anything that might get between your reader and his understanding of what you're telling him. You'll also pick up errors in grammar, syntax, subject-verb agreement, the dreaded dangling participle and the like. Each time you make any change that involves more than correcting a typo, read that part again—it's all too easy to introduce fresh errors when making corrections.

11. Check all your facts and references. Are all your quotes accurate and correctly attributed? Are the names of any experts you've quoted or referred to correctly spelled? If your piece includes instructions, measurements and the like, check that everything is accurate—no missed decimal points, no instructions given in the wrong order and so on. Don't expect the publisher's staff to do this.

12. Finish your revision by checking all the details. (Leave a day or two, or at least a few hours, before this final check.) Read each page through carefully, then read it again from the bottom line up, covering each line after you've read it. This will reveal spelling errors, repetitions of words, simple typos. When you read straight through text you tend to see what you expect to see. Reading backwards distances you from the meaning of what you're reading and makes errors much easier to spot.

13. Have you kept accurate records of all your sources of information, quotations, experts consulted etc. You might be asked to supply these—and they might be

checked out. (*Reader's Digest*, for example, checks all sources meticulously.)

### *Make a note*

- If anything at all causes you to pause in your reading, double-check it. Often our subconscious reacts instinctively, so don't ignore even the faintest warning bell.

## The cover sheet

Make sure you've put your name and address and full contact details on the first page of your manuscript. Then type out a cover sheet; this should show the title of your article, your name as author, the number of words in the article, and your name and address with your full contact details.

The editor can then send this separate cover sheet to the finance department without having the bother of copying out your details. Anything you can do to make the editor's life easier and save his time will be welcome.

## Sending an invoice

Many publications require you to send an invoice at a specified time, usually a month or so after your article is published. Clarify this beforehand with the editor who commissioned or accepted your article. You could wait forever for payment if you don't submit your bill. That's what an invoice is, a bill asking for payment. Make sure all your contact details appear on your invoice, as in the example shown in Figure 5, and keep a copy.

## Creating a master article

This is a tip from a veteran journalist who has earned a good living from his writing for many years. It's such a simple idea: collect everything you know and every bit of research on a particular topic into one master article which you keep on file. Add to this article at any time and update facts when necessary. Organise the material in whatever logical order

Jennifer Jotter  3 Market Mews  Writerton  South County  SC16 2XX
Tel: 01234 567 888   E-mail: JJotter@ISP.com

INVOICE

1st May 200X

Wilton Wordsmith
Editor
South County Times
Southern Street
Southtown ST29 1XX

To supplying one short feature 'How to be Brilliant at Everything'
550 words
Published in South County Times  27th March 200X    £25.00
=====

**Figure 5. Example of an invoice.**

you choose, but don't try to angle it to any particular market. This is a collection of facts, figures, ideas, opinions, new thinking, anything and everything relevant to this one topic. You'll have a treasury of sound up-to-date data and ideas you can turn to whenever you see an opening for a piece on that topic. Makes sense, doesn't it?

And when your master article expands beyond a few thousand words, think about it as the possible basis for a book. That makes sense, too.

## To specialise or not?

There's much to be said for specialising in a subject in which you have a strong and abiding interest, especially if you also have sound practical experience.

As a lover of books since childhood, I was overjoyed to find a job where people paid me to read books. The years in a publishing house that followed gave me the background knowledge and experience to be able to pass my own know-how on to others, in articles and books. Being well aware of the need to keep up to date, I've subscribed over the years not only to trade publications but also to writers' magazines and newsletters. If you decide to be a specialist writer, you'll need to do the same in your own niche interest. Any kind of specialist knowledge inevitably becomes out-dated.

There is no doubt that specialising gives you an inside track with editors and publishers.

Perhaps, though, you prefer variety. There are plenty of openings in all kinds of different publications—provided you can adapt your material and your style, you can do very well, and won't risk getting bored.

Whichever route you choose, the most important thing is to keep developing and polishing your writing skills.

## Pitching for a column

Most magazines use regular columns on various aspects of their core interests. These columns are often written by staff or by regular contributors. Some of these writers might be experts in their field, and some might be there because their names are well known to the public and enhance the publication's credibility and sales. Other columnists, though, are there because they have established a track record in writing about a specific subject which that publication's readers enjoy and value.

A regular column might be any length from a couple of hundred words to a thousand or two. You could write a series of 200–300 word pieces like a 'Green Living' column for a lifestyle magazine, illustrated with sketches or photographs, or you might supply a monthly 1000-word series of consumer reports focused on specific products, to give just a couple of possibilities.

If you've already published a few articles on a subject you're particularly keen on, perhaps drawn from a hobby or special interest, or your career or life experiences, you could be in a strong position to offer a column on that topic.

Whatever subject you think of offering, bear in mind that writing a column takes stamina and on-going enthusiasm. You need to have an abiding interest in your topic. If your own interest flags, your readers will notice—and your first reader is the editor.

### Make a note

- Don't commit yourself to writing on a subject you're only mildly interested in. It takes passion and true enthusiasm to sustain such an on-going project.

You might find an opening for a column in one of the magazines you've already written for. Check out your local newspaper, too—perhaps there's a gap in the coverage you could fill on a regular basis. Make sure you get a fair financial return for your work, though; many local papers are reluctant payers. If something is worth publishing, I believe it's worth reasonable payment. (There are all too many people around who are prepared to write for little or nothing, just to see their name in print. They do none of us any favours.)

To break in, you need to know your market. As with any other kind of submission, it's a waste of everybody's time to offer an editor a column on a topic that's inappropriate to his or her publication.

You also need to demonstrate that there's no risk that you might run out of steam—or ideas—after just a few columns. Reassure your target editor about this by preparing three or four complete columns, plus detailed outlines for three or four more, and one-line ideas for at least a further half-dozen.

If your proposed topic has associated products, try to ferret out some financial information to help sell your column to the editor. For example, if you write about computer games, research how much the companies who make them spend on advertising. This kind of information will help your target editor convince his or her company that your column could help sell advertising space.

Here are a few tips to help you get started:

- Know your readership. It's vital to understand the interests and concerns of the people you're writing for. Many magazines produce a media pack (as mentioned on page 44) that includes readership profiles and demographics. Some of them publish such information on their websites. Use this information to supplement your own market research and analysis.

- Know your topic inside out and from every imaginable angle. You don't need a degree to write about, for example, collecting ceramics, but you do need to know the factories, designers, identification marks, dates, auction houses, experts, restoration techniques, current values and so on.

- Focus each column on a narrow area within your subject niche. Readers want details and specific information, not generalities.

- Keep meticulous records of sources and transcripts of interviews—you might be called upon to produce them.

- Write fairly and accurately. Don't invent 'experts' or sources of quotations. Any writer who does this risks losing their credibility and their career.

- Write with authority. You know your topic thoroughly— make sure you convey your knowledge with confidence.

- Encourage your readers to write to you 'care of' the publication. (Perhaps you could offer a 'Question and Answer' section.) Answer the letters, and make sure your editor knows about them. A columnist who generates reader-correspondence is an on-going asset to the publication.

- Meet deadlines. It's a good idea to provide the editor with a few back-up columns on aspects of your topic that won't date. These can be held on file in case illness or any other unforeseeable event prevents you from delivering your column on time.

- Think ahead for seasonal aspects of your topic.

- If the magazine has a presence at events like trade shows and festivals, offer any help you can give, maybe handing out flyers or manning a subscription table.

- Accept with good grace any changes the editor makes to your column. *A little bit of advice*: If you want to challenge any change you don't agree with, have a very good reason for doing so, and plenty of ammunition to back up your argument. Remember, it will be easier for the editor to find another columnist than for you to find another regular slot.

## Don't get complacent

However well established the magazine you write for, there is no guarantee it will be there tomorrow. The magazine I mentioned earlier, *Freelance Writing & Photography*, was well known and well respected for almost four decades. As well as contributing articles, I wrote its 'agony' page for several years, dealing with readers' problems and requests for information. The magazine lasted less than a year after it was sold. With its demise went a regular part of my writing income as well as occasional fees for article contributions.

Take nothing for granted. Keep searching out and developing other outlets, other relationships. The writing business is like quicksand—you never know when a market will change or even disappear completely.

### Make a note

- The writing business is full of hazards. Don't rely on anything lasting for ever. Nothing does. Keep building your contacts and your outlets. Keep on learning.

## Keeping records—a brief reminder

Don't forget to keep all your records accurate and up to date, as we discussed in Chapter 4. You never know when you might be asked to produce them.

A track record of published articles will give you confidence in yourself and an impression of authority in approaching publishers. It will also boost your credibility if you want to approach experts for quotes and/or permission to include copyright material, should this be appropriate. The next chapter shows you what is involved.

## Points to remember

- Take care to choose the most appropriate form and style for your article.
- Study published how-to articles, and analyse how different writers work.
- Practise writing standfirsts for articles you read.
- Study sidebars that appear with published articles; note the different ways of setting out the material.
- Always prepare your manuscript in the industry standard format. Badly presented work turns editors off.
- Revise your work meticulously before submission.
- Give some thought to the possibility of specialising.
- Start creating a master article on your best subject.
- Consider trying to sell a column.
- Be alert to changes in the market—take nothing for granted.

# 8 Writing a how-to book

## Is your book idea commercially viable?

Before you embark on such a big project you need to look at your book idea objectively and assess its commercial viability. These are the questions you need to ask yourself:

- Is the topic substantial enough for a book?
- Do you have, or do you know how and where to find, enough material to fill a full-length book of at least 30,000 words without waffle or padding, packing every chapter with interesting and relevant facts? (There is scope for shorter books in children's books and gift books—see below.)
- Will the subject interest a wide enough readership to make money for the publisher?

- Will there be a demand from libraries as well as booksellers?
- How much competition is already out there? You need to know so you can
  a) avoid approaching any publisher with a similar title on his list, and
  b) alert your target publisher to competing titles.

## Assessing the competition

Note the titles and publishers of any books you already know about that might be classed as competition to the one you want to write. Then look in the yearbooks for the names of publishers who produce similar types of books, and check their websites or their catalogues for potential competition. You need to show your target publisher that you are aware of other books in the field.

If you're venturing into a popular area, your book will have to be different in some way from what is already out there. We'll look at this further below.

### Make a note

- Publishers are in business to make money. They won't take on your book if it looks like a financial risk.

## The two main types of how-to book

Which category does the book you want to write fit into, 'self-help/art of living' or 'practical'? The different types need different treatments.

Let's look first at the self-help field.

The expansion of 'self-help', 'art of living' and 'mind, body and spirit' publishing in the last half-century has been phenomenal, and shows no sign of slowing down. Where once people turned to the priest, the family doctor or a venerated family member for help with a problem, they now head for the nearest bookshop.

Self-help books on every imaginable subject are flying off the bookshelves, nourishing their readers' hopes and dreams as well as their publishers' profits.

There are literally millions of people out there searching for advice on every emotional and physical aspect of their lives. Here are just a few examples of topics you might feel inspired to write about

- How to become more creative at work, at leisure, in retirement, in finding love, in bringing up children, in coping with problems…
- How to handle the emotions that could diminish or even destroy our lives—jealousy, anger, grief, lust, greed…
- How to enjoy life at every age…
- How to cope with a phobia…
- How to be more effective in various aspects of life—in work, at play, in relationships…
- How to manage time—at work, at home, at leisure…
- How to nurture inner spirituality…
- How to build self-esteem…
- How to salve your social conscience by living a 'greener' life…

Don't imagine that because a topic has already been covered there won't be room for more—there will always be a market for a different angle, a fresh outlook, perhaps a dynamic reversal of the treatment.

To give you an example from my own experience: when I wrote my first book advising writers on how to get published, I turned the usual order of things right round. Most writers' guides at the time began by looking in detail at the writing of the genre they were covering, leaving the nitty-gritty of market study, manuscript preparation, approaching publishers and so on to a few scant pages at the end. I looked at the topic from the publisher's side of the desk, and put the business sections first. I had to put up a strong argument to convince the publisher that this treatment would work. Writers liked it, and the book has been selling steadily in its various editions for almost twenty years.

**Make a note**

● Look for fresh angles on familiar topics.

Here are just a few examples of recent books in the self-help field, to show you the scope:

*Living with the Black Dog—How to cope when your partner is depressed,* Caroline Carr

*You Didn't Hear It From Us—New York's Hippest Bartenders Tell You How to Get Your Man,* Dushan Zaric and Jason Kasmas

*Super Brain: 101 Ways to a More Agile Mind,* Carol Vorderman

*Age-Proof Your Brain: Sharpen Your Memory in 7 Days,* Tony Buzan

*You Can Be Amazing: Transform Your Life With Hypnosis,* Ursula James

*You Don't Need a Title to be a Leader: How Anyone, Anywhere, Can Make a Positive Difference,* Mark Sanborn

*You Can Stop Smoking,* Jennifer Percival

*Tactics: The Art and Science of Success,* Edward de Bono.

The other main how-to field lies in practical hands-on instruction books. We looked at this type of material in the chapters on article-writing; the advice given there holds good for books, too. This type of book works best with

● simple straightforward English
● logical step-by-step instruction
● clear explanations of 'why' as well as 'how'
● enthusiastic, encouraging and positive language.

Again, here are a few titles, to show you the range being published today:

*Dinner in a Dash—50 Dinners for 6 in 60 Minutes,* Lindsey Bareham

*House Proud—Hip Craft for the Modern Housemaker,* Danielle Proud

*Upping Sticks—How to Move House and Stay Sane,* Dr Sandi Mann and Dr Paul Seager

*The Green Self-Build Book—How to Enjoy Designing and Building your own Eco-home,* Jon Broome

*Start Mosaic,* Teresa Mills
*The Practical Picture-Framing Handbook,* Rian Kanduth
*I Love Knitting,* Rachel Henderson.

Look in any bookshop for inspirational how-to titles. Could you share your own skills and knowledge with other enthusiasts? There is always room for a great new guide, whatever your subject.

## Studying and reviewing published how-to books

I would like you to go to the library or look on your own bookshelves and choose two or three how-to books on different subjects, subjects you're interested in and know something about. You don't have to be an expert; you're simply going to look objectively at how well the author handles the topic.

Write a review of each book, assessing its value to someone who knows little or nothing about the topic. Balance the good aspects against the less sound, define what you like and what you don't like. Include the author's style of writing and overall handling of the topic in your critique. Consider whether or not you would recommend this book, if you were reviewing it for a newspaper.

This exercise will teach you more about writing a good how-to book than any amount of theoretical instruction. It will also help to clarify in your mind the qualities a publisher will be looking for in your book when you come to make your sales pitch.

### Make a note

● Keep in mind the thought that some day a reviewer will assess your book in this objective way, and remember what you learned from this reviewing exercise.

## Why you should get a contract first

One of the biggest plus factors non-fiction book-writing offers over first-time novel-writing is that you won't have to write thousands of words before you can hope to interest a publisher. Non-fiction book publishing doesn't work that way.

The usual practice is to secure an agreement with a publisher before you write more than a proposal and a sample chapter or two. To you as a first-time author this means that

1. You won't spend months researching and writing a book that might never be published.
2. You can send out your proposal to more than one publisher or agent at a time without wasting months of your time and incurring huge copying and postage costs.
3. You won't risk having to do an extensive rewrite if the publisher who wants the book asks you to change the style or the running order of the content, perhaps to fit into an established series.

The advantages to each publisher you approach are

1. he or his editorial reader can assess your idea quickly
2. he can see at once whether you can write well or not
3. he can tell from the care you've put into your proposal whether or not you might be a writer he would want to work with (a reminder of the importance of first impressions!).

As Stella Whitelaw writes in the introduction to *How to Write & Sell a Book Proposal*, 'A synopsis and the first couple of chapters is a (more) manageable possibility (than a manuscript). It's small, it's portable, it can be taken home, read on the train. And it tells the editorial reader all he wants to know. He asks himself four questions:

1. Is there a story here that I like?
2. Can this writer write?
3. Is there enough material for a whole book?
4. Would the book sell?

'A good synopsis can sell a book. You are going to give it your best shot. It's the only one you've got unless you are related to the publisher, or are his daughter's best friend.'

*Make a note*

- The professional (and most efficient) way to market your non-fiction book is to present it as a concise and easy-to-assess sales package.

Market your non-fiction book, then, with a well thought-out and carefully presented proposal, as expanded below.

But first, you have to plan your book.

# Planning your book

Suppose you want to write a book about buying, selling and collecting vintage clothing. You have a good deal of practical experience in this field, your interest having been sparked originally by your mother's skill in making over second-hand clothing in times of need. You've been a keen collector for as long as you can remember, and have spent the last five years building up a successful business as a dealer in vintage designer goods. You feel well qualified to advise other people on how to get started.

Begin by mapping out a chapter outline of the whole book, on the lines of the example shown in Figure 6:

How to Buy and Sell Vintage Clothing
by Emily Trader

**Chapter Outline**
*Chapter One*
What is 'vintage' clothing?
Why we should be interested:

- Beauty and originality of fabric and design.
- Conserving the heritage of fashion.
- It's eco-friendly to re-use garments and materials.

*Chapter Two*
Know your materials—brief chronological history of the introduction of new materials.

How to check condition.

- Will it wash?
- Will it dry-clean?
- When not to buy—how to recognise when a potential purchase is not worth the effort or the money.

Designer names to look for, by the decade—for example,

- 1920s—Chanel, Lanvin, Fortuny…
- 1930s—Schiaparelli, Vionnet…
- 1940s—Utility and rationing—from wartime to Dior's New Look…
- 1950s—Chanel again, Dior, Balenciaga, Hartnell…
- 1960s—Mary Quant, Biba, Ossie Clark…
- 1970s—Courreges, Lagerfeld, Zandra Rhodes…

### Chapter Three
Happy hunting grounds—where to find vintage clothing.
How to build contacts for regular supplies.
Buying from charity shops.
Buying at auctions.
To buy or not to buy online?

### Chapter Four
What to pay.

- How to work out your potential profit.
- How to bargain.

### Chapter Five
How to make essential repairs.

- Linings.
- Seams.
- Replacing zip fasteners.
- How to find help without breaking the bank.

### Chapter Six
How to unpick a garment.
How to remake and recycle old fabrics.
Chapter to include easy-to-use pattern templates.

**Chapter Seven**
How to price for resale.
Finding a balance to reflect your time and work without discouraging sales.

**Chapter Eight**
Where and how to sell.

- Is it worth renting shop premises?
- Selling from home.
- Selling on the internet.
- Selling at auction.

How to build a regular clientele.
To specialise or not.
How to safeguard your reputation.
To deal in furs or not?

**Chapter Nine**
Don't forget the accessories.
Shoes.
Handbags.
Jewellery.
Names to look out for.

**Chapter Ten**
Building your own collection.

**Back matter**
Glossary of terms.
Shoppers' guide.
Useful addresses.
Useful websites.
Index.

Figure 6. Example of a chapter outline for a non-fiction book.

As well as contributing an essential element to your proposal, your chapter outline gives you the bones on which to build the meat and muscle of your how-to book.

## Preparing a proposal

To market a full-length non-fiction book, you need much more than the one- or two-page letter you would send as a query about an article. You should include:

- a brief covering letter
- a succinct overview of the book in two or three sentences—a blurb, in effect
- why there is a need for the book
- who will buy the book—an assessment of the potential readership
- the competition—books on the same subject already on the market, and why your book will be different and/or better
- reasons why you are the right person to write this book, with details of any relevant qualifications. Relevance is key here; your degree in media studies won't impress an editor who is considering your book on motorcycle maintenance. Credentials that impress include
    - business or job experience
    - diplomas and degrees
    - lectures or talks given
    - publication of articles or papers on the subject
    - prizes or awards won
    - membership of relevant organisations.
- a detailed chapter outline, like the example in Figure 6.
- if your book requires illustrations, state whether or not you'll be able to supply these.

Prepare two or three sample chapters, so you're ready to respond without delay if you're asked to send them.

## House style

Every publishing house has its own style in matters like

- the use of italics or quotation marks to distinguish book and film titles and the like

- the use of 'ise' or 'ize' in verb endings
- the use or not of capital letters in, for example, Local Councillor, Inspector, Mayor and so on
- the inclusion or not of full stops after Mr, BBC, eg, ie and so on
- the spelling out or not of numbers: eleven or 11, thirty-five or 35 etc.

Your publisher will supply these details in a style sheet for you to follow in preparing your manuscript for his house. However, you might earn plus points if you write your proposal in his preferred style, which you can work out by studying some of his published books at the library. The smart writer uses any means possible to present himself as a professional.

## Why titles matter

You need a working title from the start, to identify your book throughout the marketing and writing processes. If you can come up with a snappily appropriate title right away, that's fine, but your eventual publisher will probably have other ideas.

Titles can be tricky. They can make or break your book. I've experienced this myself, with a book that was published under the title *How To Raise Funds & Sponsorship*. As this was a handbook for charity fund-raisers, I had suggested calling it *How To Raise Funds for Charity* or *How To Raise Funds for Community Projects*, but the publisher was keen to include the word 'sponsorship'.

This was only my second book, and I didn't feel confident enough to argue. Big mistake. Because there was no reference of any kind to 'charity' or 'community' in the title, the book didn't sell, in spite of excellent reviews. Many bookshops where I enquired insisted they didn't have it in stock, but it was usually there—shelved under 'Business'.

That book has been out of print for more than ten years now, but I still get a healthy Public Lending Right payment on it from library loans, proof that it's popular with borrowers.

Titles matter. Even if it means arguing your case with your publisher, make sure your title reflects what is actually between the covers of your book.

## Taking your proposal to the market

Target your proposal to the right agent or publisher. You'll waste everyone's time and brand yourself as a lazy amateur if you send a non-fiction proposal to an agent or publisher who only handles fiction, or offer a book on flower-arranging to a house that specialises in military history. (These examples probably strike you as ridiculous but, believe me, people do silly things like that all the time, to the despair of publishers.)

Research the market thoroughly. Spend however long it takes to find an appropriate publisher or agent. Consult the *Writers' & Artists' Yearbook* or *The Writer's Handbook* for listings of publishers and agents and the type of work they handle.

Browse the shelves in a large bookstore, examining published books on similar subjects. Check out related titles at the online bookstore Amazon. If you find a dozen books on how to make magic widgets, your own idea for a book on making the same kind of magic widgets might be turned down by every publisher in the universe as being superfluous to an already saturated market.

However, if you are confident that your book will revolutionise the making of magic widgets and will wipe the competition off the map, go ahead, but you'll have to present an exceptionally strong proposal to convince your target publisher that every magic-widget-maker in the country will rush to buy your book the instant it comes off the press.

## Approaching a publisher

If you have some contact with a publisher already, approach them first. If you're coming cold to the market, make a list of likely publishing houses, compiled from your research, and send a letter of enquiry to the editor responsible for non-fiction books. Look on the publisher's website, or phone the switchboard and ask for the appropriate name. Check you've got the spelling right. Don't rely on the reference books for this name. Their information might be out of date.

It's vital that you address all correspondence to a person. Anything addressed to 'The Publisher' or 'The Editor' could lie around for months till somebody gets around to looking at it.

Figure 7 below shows a simple preliminary letter, introducing yourself and your idea.

Make sure you include all your contact details. Send this letter by post *individually* to the relevant people in the first three companies and/or agents on your list, or e-mail the letter (without the reference to an sae) if that is their preferred method of approach. If you don't get a nibble after three weeks, repeat the exercise with the next three names on your list.

### Make a note

- Don't stop trying. Too many writers lose hope too quickly. Editors and agents deal with hundreds of enquiries every week. Patience and perseverance are the keys to success.

---

Dear Mr Pickem

I am planning a book provisionally titled 'Buying, Selling and Collecting Vintage Clothing', and write to ask if you would like to see my proposal for this title.

I have a life-long interest in the subject, and have been running my own successful business in this field for more than five years.

With the world's ever-growing awareness of the need to recycle and conserve materials, many people are now showing a strong interest in this kind of activity.

I note that your company publishes books on similar subjects in your 'Towards a Greener World' series, and believe that my book would suit that series well.

I enclose a stamped addressed envelope and look forward to hearing from you.

Yours truly, Verity Vert.

---

Figure 7. Example of a preliminary letter.

**123**

When a publisher or agent responds, follow up right away.

Type a brief covering letter, mentioning that you're responding to the editor or agent's request, and send it off with the summary, synopsis and outline. Mark your envelope 'Requested material'. It will be dealt with faster that way.

Keep copies of everything.

If the publisher likes your proposal, he might ask you to send two or three sample chapters. Make these as good as you can.

### Make a note

- Check everything you send for typos or grammatical mistakes. Your chances of getting further with your book rest on making a great impression at this stage.

## Proposal mistakes that can lose you a deal

1. You claim that your mother, your best friend, your writers' circle and the milkman all tell you your book is brilliant and will out-sell Harry Potter. Never forget: the only opinion that counts is that of the agent or editor. Your proposal must speak for itself.

2. You claim that there's no competition. There is always competition. Other books on your subject might be hard to find, produced by small publishing houses, old and out of date—but they will be there. To state otherwise is to raise suspicion that you can't be bothered to research the market.

3. You claim that your book will shoot straight to the top of the bestseller lists. While you need to show your enthusiasm about your project, wildly unrealistic claims will alienate any agent or publisher you approach. From long experience, they will see you as being potentially difficult to work with. They know your expectations are unlikely to be realised, and that you'll probably take your disappointment out on them.

4. You give too little information in your proposal. The agent or editor needs enough detail about the proposed book

and about you as its author to make a reasoned decision on whether to take the project further. Busy people don't have time to try to read between the lines.

5. You dress up your proposal with coloured graphics and fancy fonts in a bid to attract attention. Please don't do anything like this. Present yourself as the professional writer you aspire to be. Agents and editors loathe this kind of tricksy presentation. Their first instinct—and it's usually a sound one—is to suspect that the fancy stuff is an attempt to beef up a weak proposal.

6. Your proposal is disorganised and incoherent. Learn how to put together a strong, convincing proposal. Check your target agent or publisher's guidelines on what they want to see and how they want to see it. Your proposal is your main selling tool. It should impress by being well written and professionally presented.

Read a good book on marketing. I recommend the previously mentioned *How to Write & Sell a Book Proposal* by Stella Whitelaw, and *From Pitch to Publication* by literary agent Carole Blake.

### Make a note

- Time spent preparing an impressive proposal is time well spent. Don't ruin your chances by rushing the process.

## Getting your contract checked

The offer of a contract entitles you to apply for membership of the Society of Authors. You can join the society and have your contract checked by their experts *before you sign it.*

Do take advantage of this facility—it's vital that you understand what you're signing, and that you don't sign away any rights you should hold on to.

## Delivery dates

When you sign your contract, you'll be asked to agree and confirm a date for delivery of the complete manuscript. Don't underestimate the work involved in writing a full-length how-to book. You'll probably have to do a great deal of fact-finding and double-checking. Be sure to allow yourself plenty of time.

If you find that you're not going to be able to complete the work by the agreed date, advise your publisher as early as possible, so that he can reschedule your book. Don't wait till the last minute. It's easier all round if everyone knows what they're doing and when.

## Writing how-to books for children

Publishers who produce books for children are increasing their output of non-fiction titles significantly. A healthy growth in children's activity books is opening up new opportunities for writers who can supply attractive and appropriate material.

As with adult books, you need to have a specific idea and be able to pitch that idea convincingly to the right market. The initiative taken by A & C Black in publishing its specialised *Children's Writers' & Artists' Yearbook* has provided writers with a wealth of much-needed information on this popular and highly competitive area of publishing.

It should go without saying that you need to carry out the same meticulous research of both subject material and potential markets as you would for adult books, but it's a sad fact that far too many writers regard writing for children as an easy option. Many older writers are still writing the kind of books they themselves grew up with. They are quickly disillusioned when their offerings fly back home.

### Make a note

- You won't get anywhere in the children's market if you insist on writing the kind of material that was published when you were young. You must keep up to date.

Today's young readers are growing up in a different world from anyone old enough to be reading this book, and children's publishers have to cater for the new sophistication of this electronic media-driven age. You might sigh that these changes are regrettable, and that children should be encouraged back to cosy tales about talking bunnies and good kind fairies—and I've heard this argument supported at writers' events—but publishers are in business to cater for the market as it is, not as the older generation might wish it to be.

As Chris Kloet, editor-at-large for Walker Books, writes in the 2007 *Children's Writers' & Artists' Yearbook*, 'This is a selective, highly competitive, market-led business. As every new book is expected to meet its projected sales target, your writing must demonstrate solid sales potential, as well as strength and originality, if it is to stand a chance of being published.'

## Activity and hobby books for children

Many publishers are keen on books with interactive elements, rather than straightforward reading books.

The most successful how-to book 'for men of all ages' in the past decade is *The Dangerous Book for Boys* by Conn and Hal Igguden. Designed to encourage children to do something other than watch television or play computer games, this book is packed with suggestions like making a pinhole camera, understanding the laws of cricket, racing your own go-cart, building a tree-house, making crystals, teaching your old dog new tricks. ... Published in June 2006, by Christmas of that year it had sold almost half a million copies.

Here are a few more recent examples, to give you an idea of the current range of this type of book:

*The Young Gardener*
*The Girls' Book—How to be the Best at Everything*
*The Boys' Book—How to be the Best at Everything*
*Yes I Can! Help Save Our Planet*
*Peter Paints a Picture*
*Children's Healthy & Fun Cookbook*

Visit the children's shelves in the bookshops and make a note of publishers who are currently producing the kind of book you want to write. Look at their websites, where you'll see what new books are in the pipeline. Look, too, for publishers' guidelines. As with adult books, you need to make your pitch in exactly the way your target publisher prefers.

## The market for gift books

There's a healthy market for the small gift books often displayed at book shop till-points, supermarket check-outs and other 'impulse-buy' hot-spots. Christmas is the peak time for sales of these as stocking-fillers, as you would expect, but they do sell the whole year round. How-to titles are always popular. Priced to be temptingly affordable, these mini books usually cost between £2.50 and £4.99.

One of these sits on my desk. Titled *60 Ways to Feel Amazing*, by Lynda Field, it measures four inches by three inches (11 × 7.5 cm), has 128 pages, and is packed with morale-boosters and affirmations of around 100 words, each set over two pages, with headings like 'Take your day one step at a time', 'Accentuate the positive, eliminate the negative' and 'Be an encourager', all highly motivating, especially towards the end of a long working day.

Another favourite of mine, written for the popular humour market, is *Hot Tips for the Reluctant Housewife* by Shelagh Nugent. This one has a brightly coloured illustration on each recto page (not supplied by the author), and measures five inches by four-and-a-quarter inches (12.5 × 11 cm). There are 52 pages altogether, 26 of them text, from 100 to 200 words, giving comfort to undomesticated souls like me with unconventional and entertaining views on handling ironing, cooking, shopping, cleaning, kitchen gimmicks and more.

There's even a how-to book for your cat: *A Cat's Little Instruction Book*, by Leigh W Rutledge. This little 4.5 by 6 inches (11 × 15 cm) 128-page gem is packed with practical advice every cat should know, like 'Leave every dog with the impression that you are a lion cub who will be back to get even when you grow up', and 'Learn to watch everything, even with your eyes closed.'

If you can think up a humorous topic with wide appeal for a how-to gift book, you'll be in with a great chance—they are very popular.

Test your own potential by writing down a list of possible topics for a mini how-to book. You might surprise yourself with a brilliant new idea or a different take on a popular subject, in which case put everything else on hold while you write it. Here are a few thoughts, to get you started:

- How to talk to your cat/dog/budgie…
- How to get on with your mother-in-law/father-in-law/ sister-in-law/brother-in-law.
- How to love your little sister/brother.
- How to understand football/cricket/rugby/synchronised swimming…
- How to pull at parties.

You get the idea…

Here's a handful of titles to look at as models of how to write a how-to book. You should be able to find them in your local library.

*How to Write Short-Short Stories—A practical guide on how to write—and sell—the one-page story,* Stella Whitelaw

*The New Spend Less Revolution—365 Tips for a Better Quality of Life While Actually Spending Less,* Rebecca Ash

*People-Watching—How to Take Control by* Vernon Coleman

*You Can Be Amazing—Transform your life with hypnosis,* Ursula James (comes with a six-track hypnosis CD)

*How to be a Gardener—secrets of success,* (two volumes) Alan Titchmarsh

*Writing TV Scripts—Successful Writing in 10 Weeks,* Steve Wetton

*Successful Non-Fiction Writing,* Nicholas Corder.

Study these not only for content but for

- their encouraging, confident and energetic tone.
- their positive language.
- their layout.
- their logical, easy-to-follow sequence of information.

With a sound grasp of what makes a successful how-to book, you should now be ready to move on to writing your own…

## Points to remember

- You must be confident that your book idea is commercially viable, otherwise you won't be able to interest a publisher.
- Familiarise yourself with the different types of how-to book, so that you'll approach the right type of market.
- Reviewing a few how-to books will help you assess what works and what does not.
- Plan your book carefully and thoroughly, so that you can present a coherent and convincing proposal to a publisher.
- Approach your target publishers in a professional way, with a well-thought-out proposal.
- Don't prejudice your chances of success by making unrealistic claims about your book's worth or by offering an unprofessional-looking proposal.
- Consider your book's title carefully. It should tell readers clearly what your book is about.
- As soon as you're offered a contract, and before you sign anything, join the Society of Authors and get the contract checked by the society's experts.
- Respect the manuscript delivery date you've undertaken to meet. If you need an extension of time, ask for it well before the due date, to give your publisher time to reschedule your book.
- If you want to write for today's vibrant children's market, make sure your ideas are up to date.
- Consider writing for the gift book market—there are many opportunities there for the writer with imagination.
- Take time to study published books in both the practical and the self-help fields of how-to writing. This will be time well spent.

# **9** **Preparing your first draft**

**In this chapter**

- Researching your book—finding information from libraries, the internet and other resources
- Organising your material and your time
- Including appropriate back matter
- Understanding copyright and plagiarism
- Obtaining permission to use copyright material
- Acknowledging help

## Researching your book

### *Where to start?*

Unless you're going to write about some extremely obscure topic—in which case your audience is likely to be pretty limited—you'll probably find far more information than you could possibly accommodate in your proposed article or book. You'll need to be selective.

Plan ahead, and be clear about which area(s) of your subject you want to write about. Gardening, for example, is far too wide a topic even for a very big book. (Key 'gardening' into Google and you'll be offered 4,400,000 pages—how long would it take just to open even a fraction of that number?) Clearly, you need a much narrower focus if you are to make the best use of your time and energy.

Books, magazines, newspapers, newsletters, the internet ... there are so many information sources open to you that it will pay you to devise a plan and be ruthless about sticking to it. Research can be dangerously seductive, and if you allow yourself to be side-tracked into those all too fascinating byways your time schedule is sure to suffer.

# Sources of information

## *Books*

Books written by experts will give you the most easily accessible and comprehensive coverage of your subject. Printed books tend to go out of date, however. The information might even be out of date by the time the books reach the shops, given the length of time required for printing, binding and distributing them. How quickly they date depends on the subject they're dealing with.

E-books, supplied through print-on-demand, are more easily and quickly updated.

## *Make a note*

- Always be aware that the author of any book might be writing from a biased point of view—books by individual authors seldom look at a topic in a totally impartial way.

## *Library resources*

Unless you have a bottomless pocket and can afford to buy all the books you need, the public library will be your most valuable resource. Make friends with the staff—they'll usually be happy to help you. Consult the library's catalogue for relevant titles.

If your topic is of wide interest, the catalogue might show a bibliography, a list of works on that specific subject. Especially useful are bibliographies that include descriptions of the content of the books they list.

You can save time by getting to know the Dewey Classification system, used in most UK libraries. Books are shelved under these numbers:

000—General works
100—Philosophy
200—Religion
300—Social Sciences
400—Languages
500—Science
600—Technology

700—The arts and recreations

800—Literature

900—Geography, biography and history.

Your local library should be able to order any book published in the UK, even if that book is not part of its normal stock. You'll probably be charged a small fee for this service.

File by subject any notes you make from borrowed books, and note the book title and the relevant page number, the author's name, and the ISBN for every item.

### Make a note

- Let the staff at your local library know what you're interested in. They can be very helpful.

The books you consult will usually include in their back matter a bibliography of the works the author has consulted in his own research; these can give you further leads.

Consult *Willing's Press Guide* in the reference section of the library. This annual publication is packed with information about the hundreds of magazines published in the UK that never feature in the writers' yearbooks. You can buy it if you're rich enough—it costs hundreds of pounds—but the library should have it or be able to get it for you.

If you're working with a contract in hand, and have joined the Society of Authors, membership entitles you to apply for a ticket to the Reading Room at the British Library in London. There you'll have all the resources of one of the biggest and best libraries in the world at your fingertips.

### Amazon

The internet bookshop Amazon (www.amazon.co.uk) is a useful source of information about titles. On the Amazon home page, scroll the subject selector to 'Books', key in your topic and click 'Search' to bring up lists of available books—there is no obligation to buy. Here you'll also find books offered for sale by second-hand book dealers, especially useful if any of the books you need are out of print.

### Other ways to find books

Call in regularly at your local charity shops—most towns have several of these. Oxfam is particularly useful, as it has developed and is expanding a network of dedicated bookshops. Charity shops are mostly staffed by volunteers who are only there for a few hours a week, so you need to speak to the manager and ask him or her to keep an eye open for books on your topic—most will be happy to oblige and will keep a note of what you want along with your phone number.

Leave your contact details at second-hand bookshops, too. They'll be pleased to help you, and often have a wide knowledge of books and the book business.

Try car boot sales, jumble sales, charity events—anywhere that people might donate unwanted books. You might be lucky.

The monthly *Book and Magazine Collector* lists hundreds of books for sale and wanted, with the contact details of dozens of specialist book dealers. You can also advertise there for books you want.

### Children's reference books

Don't neglect children's reference books and encyclopedias. Here you'll find simple facts on every imaginable subject clearly and simply explained.

Make good use of the usually excellent children's section in your local library. The staff will be pleased to help.

### Make a note

- For bargain books on a wide range of subjects, it's worth having your name on the mailing list of Bibliophile Books, a mail order company issuing catalogues at regular intervals. See under 'Useful Addresses'.

### Newspapers

Newspapers offer the most up-to-date coverage and analysis available, especially in their specialist supplements. You can often find useful information on further reading and sources consulted detailed in sidebars. A byline or other credit line should tell you whether a feature has been written by a reporter or by an expert on the subject.

### Make a note

- Look in the library for newspapers other than those you normally read. Explore the supplements, especially those published with the quality papers.

### Magazines

Magazines and journals can be excellent sources of information, particularly the specialist titles. Many are so specialised you might not find them in the yearbooks. Look online for clubs and societies—most have a web presence nowadays.

*The Freelance Photographer's Market Handbook* is a good reference source for specialist but less obscure magazines. Aimed primarily at photographers wanting to sell pictures and photo-journalistic features, this is the official handbook of the Bureau of Freelance Photographers, which also publishes a monthly newsletter.

### Make a note

- Ask someone who knows. Who among your friends, acquaintances and workmates either knows your subject first-hand or might be able to give you a lead to some other expert? Don't overlook this simple and handy source of information.

## Researching on the internet

Who would have imagined, even ten years ago, that we would have such vast research resources literally at our fingertips and accessible from the comfort of our own homes. The internet is a marvel.

However, there is so much information available that we need to learn how to navigate the World Wide Web without either being afraid of its enormity or simply getting hopelessly lost.

Here are a few tips to simplify your web research:

- Subscribe to a 24/7 broadband service—this gives you fast unlimited access whenever you need it.
- Use the 'Advanced Search' facilities on your search engine. By keying in specific and tightly focused words, you'll cut out many useless leads.
- Allow yourself plenty of time to search out the information you need. Haste can lead to frustration and lack of discrimination.
- Double check everything, with other sources if possible. Remember that no one controls or filters the information that's put up on the net, so you have no guarantee that anything is 100 per cent reliable.
- The free online encyclopedia Wikipedia (www.wikipedia. org) can give you leads to information, publications and experts on your topic, but be aware that this site can be edited by anyone at any time. Always double check.
- Always keep your virus protection up to date.
- Invest in 'firewall' protection to fend off hackers.

### Know when enough is enough

It's all too easy to get carried away and forget you have a book to write. Research can be seductive. You need to be firm and resist all those interesting byways that invite you to explore them. Keep your research focused or you could upset your timetable.

Don't make the mistake, either, of trying to cram all your research into your book. Be selective. File the research that doesn't strictly fit this project—there might be another book there.

## Organising your material

You'll save yourself a lot of time and frustration if you sort your research material into a manageable system from the start. There are no rules about what kind of system you should use. You need to devise a method to suit the kind of book you're writing and the way you like to work. Whatever kind of how-to you're working on, you're likely to accumulate many and various bits of research. Without a system, you could easily get into a muddle and waste precious writing time searching for that essential bit of information.

My own system is simple—a set of document wallets, one for the prelims (the title page, contents etc), one for each chapter, and one for the back matter. I label each wallet clearly with the name of the book and the chapter number or section name. Each wallet might hold any number of envelopes containing, for example, cuttings, jottings of all those precious ideas, references to books I want to consult, names and contact details of people I want to speak or write to, paragraphs roughed out in a spare few minutes ... anything relevant to that particular chapter.

I don't store any research or notes solely on computer. Apart from the possibility of a technical mishap wiping everything out, it isn't always convenient to boot up the machine just to find one or two pieces of information.

This system has served me well over many years of writing how-to books and articles. You might prefer a different way. But please do organise your material. I learned the hard way, and very early in my career, that throwing everything into one shoe box doesn't work.

### Make a note

- Please do take the trouble to back up *all* your computer files on rewritable CDs or on an external memory disk. Label your back-up disks clearly and keep them in a separate place, preferably in another room. Many a good piece of writing has been lost because its author couldn't be bothered to back-up their material.

## Organising your time

Every writer needs a servant. Someone to cook the meals, see to the laundry, clean the house, pick the kids up from school—what bliss. However, few are rich enough for such an indulgence, so the rest of us have to fit our writing into whatever time we can find outside our jobs and other commitments.

You can't stretch time, or bend it, or slow it down. It doesn't fly or drag or stop. It just ticks on relentlessly. It's up to us to organise ourselves to make the best possible use of it.

You can fit the writing of short material like articles, fillers and tips into a few minutes here and there in your day, but writing a book will take a hefty chunk of your time.

Unless you're lucky enough (or successful enough) to be able to write full-time, organise your life so that you have at least one morning or afternoon a week to call your own, uninterrupted.

Read Mark Forster's book *Get Everything Done and Still Have Time to Play*—it's packed with good ideas for time-management. Mark writes in his introduction to the book that he believes our work suffers if we don't find time to play, and that 'working in a concentrated and purposeful way is less stressful than working in a distracted or unfocused way …' It takes planning and organisation to achieve this focus.

## Including appropriate back matter

Look at the back pages of almost any non-fiction book (other than gift books) and you're likely to find supporting material like explanatory notes, a glossary of terms, recommended reading, appropriate societies and associations, useful websites, an index and so on. These supplementary pages are called 'back matter', and are an essential part of any but the most basic how-to book.

It's particularly important to include an index in a book that includes references of any kind. Unless your book is highly complicated and technical, you can easily prepare the index yourself, saving the publisher (or yourself) the expense of hiring a professional indexer. See how to do it in Chapter 10.

## Understanding copyright

Copyright law protects your work during your lifetime and for 70 years after your death. In the UK, you don't have to register copyright. Anything you write is protected as soon as it's written. Your copyright is your intellectual property. No one has the right to reproduce your work in any way without your permission. You can sell your copyright in a work outright if you want to, but you would then have no further claim on money made from that work in any way.

### Make a note

- Hold on to ownership of your copyright. It's a valuable intellectual property.

Copyright law works both ways. While it protects your work from infringement by other writers, it also prohibits you from infringing the copyright of others. You can't quote any substantial part of someone else's writing, either, without permission. Such permission should be sought from the publishers of the work you want to quote from, not directly from the author (unless the work is self-published, of course). Fees can be pretty heavy, too. You can look up quotation fees in the current edition of *The Writer's Handbook*.

The Society of Authors publishes a useful *Quick Guide to Copyright*. Like all their other Quick Guides, this is free to members and available to non-members for a small fee. See the society's website at www.societyofauthors.org, where you'll find a complete list of their publications, with prices.

Non-members can also subscribe to the society's quarterly journal *The Author*—see the society's website.

### Make a note

- Be wary of quoting from letters. Under copyright law, the letter belongs to the recipient *but* the words it contains belong to the writer. Don't get caught out.

## Understanding plagiarism

Plagiarism is the use without permission of work in which the copyright is held by someone else. However much you admire a writer, and feel that their writing is in sympathy with your own, and maybe think they express your own thoughts better than you can, beware. You are breaking the

*Rock Me Gently*

The reference to Judith Kelly's book, *Rock me Gently*, concerns a first edition where 30 000 books were published containing material that was said to be taken from other books. Subseqent editions of Ms Kelly's books have had this material removed.

law if you make unauthorised use of their words in your own work.

The Society of Authors has reported a recent rise in cases of plagiarism. One of the most blatant cases to hit the headlines in recent times was that of Kaayva Viswanathan's novel *How Opal Mehta Got Kissed, Got Wild, and Got a Life*. Hailed as a prodigy at just seventeen and signed up to a six-figure advance and with a two-book deal signed and film rights sold, the Harvard undergraduate's 'coming of age' novel about a young Asian woman was exposed to her publishers as a compilation of ideas and extracts from other authors' work. Her contract and film deal were cancelled, the advance had to be returned, and the young author's chances of ever being considered by another publisher are precisely zero.

Another recent example is Judith Kelly's memoir *Rock Me Gently*. Among the top authors whose writings were plagiarised in Kelly's book were Graham Greene and Hilary Mantel.

Whether you're writing fiction or fact, take care not to try to pass off another author's words as your own.

Be careful about titles, too. If you call your self-help book by the same title as a well-known one like, for example, *Feel the Fear and Do It Anyway* or *How To Win Friends and Influence People* you could be accused of making an attempt to mislead the buying public. In law, this is termed 'Passing off'. This can be a particular hazard for self-publishers, who don't have the restraining hand of a publisher to alert them to the dangers.

## Obtaining permissions

If you want to include material in which you don't hold the copyright, you're likely to be responsible for obtaining permission from the copyright holder or holders, and for the payment of any fees such permission requires, and for any legal costs incurred if you include copyright material without clearance of permission. Check your contract: this responsibility will be spelled out there, so you have no excuse.

*Make a note*

- Read your contract clause by clause. It's your responsibility to know exactly what you are undertaking when you sign it. Ignorance is no defence in law.

# Acknowledging help

If someone has given you substantial help with your book, perhaps by obtaining research material or giving you leads to information, or by giving you helpful advice, you might want to thank them publicly for their time and trouble.

The usual way to do this is to write a paragraph or two under the heading 'Acknowledgements'. Such a notice is usually placed prominently in the prelims. (Including it in the back matter could diminish its value in the eyes of the reader.) People do like to be acknowledged—and you might want to enlist their help again in the future.

Remember, too, to give your acknowledged helpers a signed copy of your book as soon as it's published.

*Now write your book*

You have everything you need to hand, so you can now go ahead and write the whole book, building on the chapter outline you prepared for your sales package.

When you've completed the full draft, put the work aside for a few days, then come back to it fresh, ready to revise and rewrite where necessary.

## Points to remember

- Use every available method of research, but don't be seduced into spending too much time looking at irrelevant material.
- Use your local library to the full. Enlist the help of the staff.
- Look at reference books for children; their material will be meticulously researched and clearly laid out.
- Newspapers and magazines offer up-to-date information.
- Use the internet for research, but double check everything with other resources.
- Keep your research information well organised.
- Organise your writing time to best effect.
- Remember to include essential back matter.
- Be aware of copyright law, and take care not to plagiarise other people's writing.
- Be sure to obtain written permission before you quote any substantial amount of copyright material.

# 10 Revising and rewriting

*Take a short break*

Now you've completed a full draft of your book, take time to review the whole thing objectively. Ideally, you'll have built enough time into your schedule to allow you to set the work aside for at least a few days. You need a bit of space between completing the draft and starting your revision. You can then come back to the book with a fresh eye, able to see flaws that you might otherwise be too close to the work to spot.

Begin your revision with a broad view.

## Checking your book's structure

Look at the overall structure of your book. Ask yourself these questions:

- Are you happy with the balance you've given your book? Check that you haven't concentrated too much on any particular aspect—perhaps one you most enjoy writing about—and maybe given some other part less than full treatment.

- Have you set out your chapters in the most logical order, the order that will give your reader the most benefit?
- Within your chapters, have you set out the sections in the best order?

Don't be afraid to tear your book apart and restructure it if you feel this would improve its clarity and value to the reader. With the boon of computer technology, such a major piece of work would take time and care but should hold no terror. Do it if you must. Just be careful not to lose any vital component in the process.

If you do make major changes, print out another draft so you can lay everything out in front of you for another review.

When you're satisfied you have everything in the best order, move on to checking the detail.

### Make a note

- Work at your manuscript till you're completely satisfied that it fulfils everything you promised in your proposal. It will be too late to do this when your book is at the proof stage.

## Accuracy matters

In any kind of non-fiction book, it's important to get facts and figures right. With a how-to book, especially one that includes practical instructions, methods, quantities, measurements and so on, accuracy is vital. A misplaced decimal point, an inaccurate quantity, an instruction that's vague or given in the wrong order—any kind of carelessness can destroy your readers' trust in everything you've told them.

The most colourful illustration I've seen of this problem is given in the *Writer's Digest Handbook of Magazine Article Writing*, second edition, in a section titled *How To Write How-To Articles*. (All the authors are listed at the end of this handbook, but their contributions are not individually attributed, which is a shame.) This particular piece begins with a paragraph describing an officer about to disarm a bomb, following instructions given over the radio by a bomb disposal expert. "'Cut the green wire,' the expert commanded. The officer gingerly took the green wire between the jaws of his cutters and … began to squeeze. As the cutters bit through the insulation, the bomb expert's voice crackled over the handset: "But first. …'"

You're unlikely to be writing about bomb disposal, but whatever your topic, it's essential that you check and double-check that you've given the instructions in the right order.

### Make a note

- Check that you've given all the instructions necessary to complete the project, and that they are all in precisely the right order.

### Make sure your meaning is clear

Check that you have explained the meaning of every term you've used that is even slightly technical. What seems clear and straightforward to someone accustomed to the subject might be impenetrable to the novice.

### Make a note

- Unless you're writing for a specialist magazine, avoid technical terms where possible. When such terms are necessary, explain them clearly.

## Editing and polishing your text

Work through your manuscript and check the following:

- Syntax—make sure you've said exactly what you mean to say, in a clear and unambiguous way.
- Grammar—if your grammar is shaky, invest in a good handbook.
- Punctuation—check this thoroughly. Read the text aloud if you have any doubts. A misplaced comma can alter the entire meaning of a sentence.

- Spelling—don't rely on a computer spellcheck; it won't pick up correctly spelled words used wrongly, like 'their' instead of 'there', 'buy' instead of 'by' and the like.
- Paragraphing—check that your paragraphs follow on in a logical way, and that you've ensured the 'flow' by using connecting words and phrases like 'It follows, then, that …', 'If so, you might think …' and the like.
- Overall arrangement of material—check again that your chapters, and every point within the chapters, are arranged in the most logical and easy-to-follow order possible. This is the time to make any major changes, *not* after your book is typeset.
- Know when to stop. Don't edit the life out of your work.

### Make a note

- This stage offers you the last chance to make major changes. Make sure everything you want to include is there, in the right order, and correct down to the last full stop.

## Numbering your pages

Now your manuscript is complete, every detail checked, and every necessary correction made, you can insert the page numbers. Your pages should run from 1 on the title page right through to the last page of the index. Do not number your chapters separately.

You're now ready to print out your manuscript ready for submission to your publisher. He will have told you how he wants to receive the work—if not, call him and check. He might want more than one hard copy, and he'll certainly want an electronic copy. Print out a hard copy for yourself at the same time. You'll need a copy on paper to enable you to work on your index (see below). It's also useful to have a copy to hand in case your publisher calls you with a question.

## Preparing a simple index

An index is essential to your how-to book. Your reader will want to be able to find any item quickly and easily without having to waste time searching through the pages for a book title, a technique, a set of instructions or anything else he wants to refer to.

And your publisher will bless you if you can supply the index yourself, saving him the time and expense of farming out the job to a professional indexer.

You can do the basic preparation while you're writing your book. Working on a computer, it's a simple process.

When you start working on your final draft, open a separate document and make an entry there for every item you want to include in your index. Keep the entries in alphabetical order. You'll include this document in your final submission, so that your publisher will be able to include the necessary pages in his calculations of the eventual length of your book.

During the time between delivering your manuscript to the publisher and receiving your set of proofs for correction, you can place provisional page numbers into the index. It takes time and care, but it isn't difficult to do, and will save you valuable time at the proof stage, when you'll be expected to fill in the correct page numbers on the index proof.

Working on your own hard copy of the manuscript, follow these simple steps:

1. Using a coloured highlighter, work through your hard copy marking every item that appears in your draft index and, at the same time, noting the page number(s) against the item in the index. It's important to complete this step before you receive your proofs for correction, because you'll have only a limited time to read and correct them.

2. At the proof-correction stage, when you've finished correcting your proofs, mark the page numbers as they appear on the proofs on to all your manuscript pages. To do this, take a ruler and draw a line on the manuscript page to show where the page division occurs in the proofs. Indicate *exactly* where the pages divide, drawing a cut-off line as shown in Figure 8 on page 148. In this example, the page reference to *The Rag Doll Handbook* would be '103' in your typescript; in the corrected index the page reference would be '96'. The page reference to

---

McCallum| Fundraising| 103|

the many excellent books that are currently available. There are books in the shops and libraries about every imaginable craft. The following books are particularly good for the types of crafts that sell well at fairs:

The *Rag Doll Handbook* by Ana Lakeland. Sold in some of the world's most exclusive toy shops, Ana Lakeland's rag dolls are surprisingly simple to make and require only the most basic sewing skills. The book gives detailed patterns for the basic doll and for a really imaginative selection of variations including Snow White and the Seven Dwarfs, Santa Claus, sailors, / clowns and punks, and many more. (96) Included are instructions for making a box which could be used to display the dolls, or sold with them as a gift box.

*Making Silk Flowers* by Anne Hamilton and Kathleen White. This is a

---

**Figure 8. How to complete index pagination.**

*Making Silk Flowers* would be '103' in the typescript, and you would correct this in the index proofs to '97'.

3. Work through your manuscript again from the first page of text, this time correcting the page numbers in your alphabetical list so that they now correspond to the new page numbers as you've marked them from the proofs.

4. Finally, check that you have all the items listed correctly in alphabetical order, with any cross-references in place.

## Counting your words

Whatever its subject, your how-to book will be packed with advice, encouragement and information. Your text will be set out, ideally, in easily digested sections with short paragraphs. These are likely to include a fair number of bulleted segments. There will be few, if any, long discursive paragraphs. Today's readers like brevity. There will be a lot of 'air' in your text.

I would like you to do this simple exercise: Go to your bookshelves and take down half a dozen different books. Open them at random and look at the pattern of the words and lines on the pages. Unless you've chosen a deep and intense novel or a serious treatise, you'll find very few pages where there is solid text from top to bottom. Your how-to book, by its nature, won't be like that. How many lines do you see where the words don't occupy the full width of the text? How many side headings are there, likewise containing only a few words? Most books that are easily readable have a good deal of white space on the pages.

You can see, then, that relying on your computer program's word count to tell you how long your book is going to be could be a big mistake. The word count facility only counts the words. It doesn't make allowances for the white space left by those short lines at the end of paragraphs, those bullet point lists, those subheadings, those indented sections. Yet a line containing a short sub-heading or one with only one or two words occupies the same amount of space on the page as a full line of text.

Here, then, is a simple way to work out the overall word count for your book manuscript:

1. Count only full lines of text.
2. Count the number of words in a total of ten *full* lines on one page (you'll probably have to jump from paragraph to paragraph to do this). Make a note of that number of words.
3. Do the same count with nine more batches of ten lines from pages at intervals throughout your manuscript.
4. Add together all ten results to give you the total number of words you've counted.
5. Divide this total by 100.
6. This gives you the average number of words per full line of your text.
7. Now count the number of lines of text in your whole manuscript, including all short lines and part lines. (If you've kept the number of lines per page reasonably even, you should be able to arrive at this total by multiplying the total number of pages by the average number of lines per page.)

8. Finally, multiply the total number of lines by the average number of words per line. Round this figure up to the nearest 1000.

This wordage total gives your publisher the information he needs to decide on the type font (the design of typeface) and type sizes, the area of text on the page, the margin sizes and so on, to give him the number of printed pages he wants to see in the finished book.

## Dealing with copy-editing changes

Depending on your publisher's resources, he might send a copy of your manuscript to a professional copy editor. Many publishing houses nowadays use freelance copy editors. Few can afford to support enough staff in-house.

The copy editor's job is to check your manuscript line by line (in the US, the designation is 'line editor'), and make any necessary corrections to your spelling, syntax, grammar and so on. They should refer anything more major to you via the publisher, as a query. It should not be within their brief to make any major alterations to your text without checking them out with you.

I have worked as a freelance copy editor for several major publishers, and always respected the author's wishes, as I was trained to do in my early days in publishing. However, as an author myself, later in my career, I have had to argue my case quite vigorously with copy editors who have worked on my books. Sometimes they can be over-eager to put their own stamp on your work, and might also feel obliged to make changes simply to justify their employment. Have the courage to stand up for yourself if changes are suggested—or made—that you disagree with and are able put up a strong case against. It's your book, after all, not theirs.

## Proof-reading

Your publisher will send you a set of proofs for correction. He should tell you what colour ink he wants you to use to mark your corrections and any essential alterations. The usual system is to use red marks for printer's errors and blue marks for author's corrections, but be guided by your publisher's wishes on this.

Note that word, 'essential'. Proof correction is not an invitation to rewrite sentences, change your mind about the running order, or move chunks of text around. At this stage in your book's production, corrections can be expensive to make, especially if they involve changes to the running headlines and the page numbering. Check your contract: you're likely to be charged with the costs if you make too many unnecessary changes.

Go through your proofs with meticulous care. This is your last chance to correct any errors in the text. Mark the changes as clearly as you can, using the standard proof correction marks. You can find these in the *Writers' & Artists' Yearbook*, well set out and easy to understand.

Here's a useful proof-reading tip to help you pick up as many mistakes as possible: Read each page carefully from first line to last, then read it again *from the bottom up*, starting with the last line and, with a sheet of paper, covering up the lines you've read. This trick makes you look at the words out of their context, and shows up errors you might easily miss in a straightforward read-through. When we read, we read the meaning of the words, and we see what we expect to see. Try it—it works.

## Paperless proofs

By the time your book is at the proof stage, your publisher might be using the latest computer technology to provide 'paperless proofs' for you to correct on-screen.

This is a highly effective way to save time, paper and postage costs. It's a truly 'green' advance, and you can see how it works by logging on to www.paperlessproofs.com. Watch the demonstration and be amazed.

## Registering your book for Public Lending Right

This is a right for which writers fought long and hard. It's a scheme that rewards authors for loans of their books made through public libraries. If you would like to know more about the history of the scheme and how it works, visit the PLR website at www.plr.uk.com.

Register your book for Public Lending Right as soon as it's published. Registration entitles you to a small payment for each loan of your book from a public library, calculated on loans from a representative sample of libraries across the UK. It's worth doing, and costs you nothing. My how-to books have earned a useful three-figure payment every year since publication.

### Make a note

● Do take the trouble to register for PLR. If you don't bother, you could miss out on your payment entitlement. There is no automatic registration.

## Self-publishing—is it for you?

Publishing your own book can be an exciting venture. It can also be a big risk. You need to weigh the advantages against the hazards:

In your favour:

● Your book will get published
● Your book will get published quickly
● Your book will look exactly as you want it to look
● You control the editing
● You control the production
● You control the marketing
● You handle the accounts
● You get all the profits.

On the hazard side:

● You bear all the expense
● You make all the decisions
● You invest countless hours of your time
● You have to pay people to do any of the tasks you can't do yourself
● You have to market the book yourself
● Any financial loss will be yours and yours alone.

Self-publishing can be a lot of fun, and it can make you a lot of money. Mainstream publishers sometimes make an offer for a self-published book that has attracted good reviews and looks like generating healthy sales. Don't take this possibility into account, though, when you're calculating the risks. It might not happen to you.

### Can you afford the time and the financial outlay?

How much of a risk-taker are you? Answer these questions honestly—don't lie to yourself.

- Do you have the right temperament for such a risky venture?
- How much time and work are you prepared to put into the project?
- How much faith do you have in your book?
- Are you a good sales-person?
- And the crunch question: Can you afford to lose *all* the money you've invested in the project if the book fails to sell?

Apart from the financial risk, you should also take into account the possible emotional and psychological damage you might suffer if your venture fails. Don't go down the self-publishing road without a lot of thought—it's not for the faint-hearted.

If you would like a 'warts and all view of self-publishing', as he describes it himself, read Vernon Coleman's book *How To Publish Your Own Book*. Vernon Coleman is a legend in the publishing world. Since 1975, he has been publishing his own books successfully under his own imprint, Blue Books. He writes mostly non-fiction and focuses mainly on health and well-being, but he has also self-published several novels.

If you need a self-publishing guru, this is the man. Look out for his adverts in national papers and magazines—he's a marketing genius. If you're giving serious consideration to publishing your own book, do get his book. It's the best I know on the subject.

### *Make a note*

- Don't risk self-publishing if you can't afford to lose your money. It's a big risk.

The Society of Authors—always reliable—publishes a *Quick Guide to Self-Publishing.* See their website.

In the next chapter, we'll look at the possibilities offered by writing in collaboration with other people.

## Points to remember

- Give yourself enough time to review and revise your manuscript objectively.
- Be aware of how a copy editor works—and be prepared to argue your case if changes are made that you don't like.
- Preparing a simple index is not difficult but takes time and care.
- Read your proofs conscientiously and carefully. The quality of your book is your responsibility as much as your publisher's.
- Don't be tempted to make major changes at proof stage; you could be asked to meet the costs.
- Register your book for Public Lending Right as soon as it's published. You're entitled to the appropriate financial reward if your book is widely borrowed from public libraries.
- If you're considering self-publishing, read all you can about the subject, and take time to balance the rewards against the risks.

# 11 Working with a collaborator

Many excellent books are produced by writers working with experts in some form of collaboration. When such a partnership gels, two minds can be many times better than one, each sparking off the other and melding individual skills into a far more exciting book or article than either partner could have written alone.

## Getting started

Try breaking into the market with a strong 'as told to' piece. Much loved by women's magazines, these are true-life human interest stories told in the first person by the 'writer'. Titles like 'I helped my daughter conquer bulimia' and 'I lost half my body weight and found true love' are the bread and butter of the women's weeklies. (Did you spot the missing word in each of these titles? These are how-to pieces in all but name.)

These really are true stories. Sometimes the names are changed in the printed piece, to protect the subject's privacy, but the stories are not made up. We live in a different world from that of the old 'sin, suffer and repent' confession stories, most of which were pure fiction.

So how do you find these stories? To find people with fascinating experiences that others would love to read about, you can

- Let friends and acquaintances know what you're looking for and ask them to put you in touch with possible subjects.
- Keep searching your local paper for news of people who have done interesting things. To contact a person you don't know, write to the paper's editor, asking for your enclosed letter to be sent on. Stamp the enclosure but leave it unsealed, so that the editor can see it's a genuine approach—ask him to seal it before sending it on.
- Listen to your local radio—especially phone-in programmes. Make your approach as above, via the programme's producer.
- Get involved in voluntary work. Spend a few hours a week working behind the counter in a charity shop or a hospital café and you'll hear more human interest stories than you could ever handle.
- Read the national newspapers. In these days of fast communications, you don't need to have your subject on the doorstep.

Once you've made contact, arrange to meet your subject if you can. You can then use the interviewing techniques we looked at in Chapter 5 to get the full story and—most important—anything more your subject can tell you that will help other people learn from their experience. Get as much information as you can about support groups, sources of advice and so on. You can supplement this information later from further research.

Write the piece up in the first person, as if your subject were telling his or her own story. The heading will byline the article to your subject by name, as in "'I saved my marriage by living on lettuce and lemon juice for six months!" says Bobby Brave', while your own credit will appear at the end: 'as told to Jennie Scribe'.

When you're writing this kind of piece, it's important to remember that the reader is less interested in the experience for itself than in how that experience reflects his or her own life and problems. You might want to include a supplementary paragraph or two giving specific advice to the reader on how to cope with the problem as it affects their own life.

## Writing up other people's experience, skills and know-how

Most of us know at least one or two people who have skills and experience the rest of us envy.

Perhaps your neighbour grows prize-winning bonsai or paints beautiful watercolours. Maybe your office colleague wins every golf tournament in the county or makes delicious wine from his own hothouse grapes.

Any and all of these skills could interest a wide enough readership to make them subjects for saleable articles.

Get your notebook out and make a list of people you know whose know-how you could write up—and start making calls.

## Collaborating on a book—the pleasures and pitfalls

Writing an article with someone else is stimulating and interesting—and short-term. You won't be committing yourself to spending a hefty chunk of time on the project.

Before you commit yourself to writing a book with another person, however, you need to be aware of the risks. This is not like going out on a dinner date, when you can go your separate ways if you find you don't enjoy each other's company as much as you thought you would.

Writing a book means working closely with this person for many months, possibly years. You want to be sure the relationship will work.

You need to meet any potential collaborator in person before you sign any agreement. You might take an instant dislike to them, or they to you. It's essential that you spend a few hours together, share a meal, talk the project through, even if you have to travel some distance to do this.

You'll be making a big investment in this person, not only in time but in money, too, if the project prevents you from earning in other ways. You could also be risking your reputation.

### Make a note

- It's advisable that both parties in a writing partnership should conduct themselves professionally at all times. If you become too casual and friendly you could find it difficult to sort out disagreements. Keep the relationship cordial and relaxed but fairly formal.

If your proposed collaborator is a craftsman, check out the quality of his products, and his reputation among fellow craftspeople. Someone who wants you to help them write a book on 'My Castle in Spain—How I Built my Dream House on the Costa Lotta' should be able to produce plans, photographs, licences, testimonies from Spanish neighbours and the like.

If she is a psychologist or a scientist or a medical expert, check her qualifications. Wherever this person's expertise lies, find out as much as you can about them. Look them up on the internet, ask people who know them, check their credentials with professional or academic associations.

You can learn a lot more about someone by spending a few hours in their company, though. The ideal collaborator will be

- friendly but businesslike
- happy to answer your questions about his qualifications—see below
- decisive, not waffly
- sensible about the business aspects of the deal

- happy to sign a contract with you
- willing to help with promotion
- reliable to work with
- ideally, living near enough to allow regular meetings.

The last point is not as important as it once was. E-mail has made contact so much easier and quicker, you could probably conduct the whole business without ever meeting again. That first face-to-face meeting is essential, though.

You'll have to rely a lot on instinct. If you feel that this is a partnership that might not work, don't take it any further. Be wary of someone who is over-friendly, who wants to confide details of his personal life, emotional problems and so on. You're looking for a business associate, not a new best buddy.

# Finding an expert

There are various ways you can find a potential collaborator:

1. Find them in person. People love to talk about themselves and what they do. If you meet an interesting person at a social or business event, encourage them to talk and if you see possibilities in what they tell you, sound them out on how they feel about a professional relationship.
2. If you have a specific area of interest in mind, ask the librarian at your local public library—they might keep information about experts in various fields for the convenience of researchers.
3. Read magazines on the topics you're interested in. Look for leads to experts in articles and references. Look also at the credits against the names of the editorial staff and regular contributors.
4. Go to places where you might expect the experts to go: exhibitions, talks, presentations and so on.
5. Ask at local colleges, universities, evening classes—most of the lecturers and tutors are experts in their fields.
6. If you want to get in touch with a published author who doesn't have a website or who doesn't offer contact details, write to them 'care of' their publisher. Most publishers are meticulous about passing on such letters.

## Making it easy for the expert to find you

Spread the word among all your contacts that you're open to suggestions for collaborative writing.

1. Post your details on your website if you have one.
2. Advertise your availability locally and in *The Bookseller*, the publishing trade 'organ', or in *Publishing News*.

### Make a note

It's important to check these points

- Is your would-be collaborator really an expert and not just someone who thinks he is or who would like to be?
- If he has paper qualifications, how up to date are they?
- If this is a retired person, how up to date is he with developments in his field?

## Working out the agreement

Before you do any substantial work on your project, you need to prepare a written agreement that both parties are happy to sign. Some aspects of this agreement could affect the eventual contract you and your collaborator will sign with a publisher. Establish the ground rules from the start. You don't want to be involved in arguments about what was agreed and what was not after you've put months of time and work into the project.

### The credits

In a collaboration, as distinct from a ghost-written book (see below), your name as the writer, and your collaborator as the expert, should have equal prominence. The expert's name usually comes first, as the book is about his subject. The credit could read either

How to Live For Ever
by
A N Optimist and A Penman

or

How to Live For Ever
by
A N Optimist with A Penman

There is a subtle difference here. The first version puts your name and the expert's on an equal footing. The second implies that your part in the project is slightly less important than the expert's. In your own interest, hold out for the first version.

## Copyright and royalties— safeguarding your interests

Make it clear at the start that you want a 50–50 share in everything. Anything less will be a bad deal for you, as you'll be doing the bulk of the work. Someone who has never written a book won't be able to understand how much work, know-how and sheer sweat goes into putting all those thousands of words together.

If your expert is someone famous, or well known in a particular field, they might believe they are more important than you are. Be as tactful as you can, but make it clear that your skill in writing the book is just as important as their expertise in the subject. It's a joint venture. You should share the benefits equally.

If your expert tries to insist on having more than a 50 per cent share in any area, you would be wise to think the implications through, and to walk away if you feel you're being manoeuvred into an unfair deal. No relationship can work smoothly if one party feels hard done by.

Take the same care over the eventual publishing contract. You want to safeguard your share of both the royalties earned and your copyright interest, so that you get your fair share of any subsidiary rights that might be sold.

### Make a note

- In the writing world, you don't get what you deserve, you get what you negotiate.

- Don't take on a joint venture unless you are totally happy with the terms agreed. Small resentments could grow too big to handle if things begin to go wrong.

## Registering for your share of Public Lending Right

Both you and your collaborator must register your book individually for Public Lending Right. The registration form will ask you to state the percentage of the due payment you're claiming. With your 50–50 deal, this would mean each of you claiming 50 per cent of any PLR payment due. You can only register to claim your own share. You can't claim on behalf of the other person, and vice versa.

Forms are available to download from the PLR website, www.plr.uk.com, or you can ask for them by writing to the PLR office. Whether you download the form or get it by post, you're required to sign it after completion and return it by post.

## Ghostwriting—what it involves

'Ghostwriting' is a term used when someone writes something for a client and the client gets the full credit for it.

The reading public is generally unaware of how many books are written by 'ghosts'. A substantial proportion of the books on the best-selling lists at any given time are ghostwritten.

A ghostwriter writes articles, books, manuals, e-books and mini-courses for the internet, speeches for other people—and how-to material. You can earn a lot of money as a ghostwriter, but you won't earn fame. Your name won't appear on the work except when you're occasionally acknowledged as 'editor' or 'proof-reader', thanked for 'help with the manuscript' or the like. Don't expect any kind of benefit other than money when you're starting out.

Occasionally, a ghostwriter becomes so well known that his or her name on the cover of a book will be regarded as a marketing asset. Andrew Crofts, for example, has ghosted so many big-selling books and has built up so much credibility in the publishing world that his name often appears now as co-author; *Betrayed* 'by Lindsey Harris with Andrew Crofts' sits high in the non-fiction best-seller lists as I write. Such prominence takes many years to achieve, though.

Andrew has advertised his ghostwriting services in the trade papers for many years, and is also the author of *The Freelance Writer's Handbook* where he includes a chapter on ghostwriting. In that chapter, he comments,

'Most people in a position to require a ghostwriter can almost certainly command larger fees for their words than the people who do the ghosting for them. They'll probably be able to sell more books as well. As a result there will be more money in the pot and the ghost's share is always likely to be more than he or she could earn by writing the book on their own.'

My own experience of ghostwriting a book proved that last point. I was hired to ghost an autobiography by someone who had an interesting story to tell involving plenty of travel and a 'forbidden' marriage that put both parties in great danger. I found the job demanding but enjoyable and I learned a lot about two very different cultures. The best part, though, was the money.

This private individual paid top rates to have the story written before any publisher's contract was secured. For that reason I worked on a flat fee basis, signed the copyright over to the 'author' on completion and walked away with my big fat cheque. It was the biggest single payment I had earned in years.

## Beware the pitfalls

If you venture into ghostwriting, you should be aware of potential problems. Here are a few tips to remember:

- Always have a properly drawn-up agreement. If there is going to be a substantial sum of money involved, have the agreement drawn up by a professional. Each party must have a copy, signed by both client and ghostwriter.

- Make sure you're going to have enough access to and contact with the client. Include this requirement in the agreement, worded so that denial of adequate access by the client will void the contract. You need to be ruthless about this, otherwise you could waste hours of your writing time on an elusive and uncooperative client.
- Make sure you don't get tied into an over-tight time schedule. Insist on adequate time. Non-writers have little understanding of the time and effort involved in writing. It's up to you to assess the time you'll need.
- Unless you've been commissioned to do this work by a publisher or agency, in which case the publisher or the agency will be paying you, be wary of making any agreement with your client that does not guarantee you'll be paid for your time and effort. Reject any suggestion that you'll write the book for a share of the eventual profits—there might not be any profits. The book might never be published.
- Make no promises to the client. You know the publishing business, he doesn't. No writer can guarantee publication of any work till there is a publishing contract on the table. You won't have any control over the acceptance or rejection of the work. You can offer to help by writing model letters and perhaps a synopsis, and by showing the client how to pitch the work to publishers. (You should be paid extra for this.) However, as above, the book might never be published.
- Don't assign copyright in the work to the client until you receive payment in full for the work you've done. Every word you've written is legally yours till you surrender the copyright in writing.

## Finding clients

Here are a few suggestions on how to spread the word that you are available for ghostwriting work. You can

- Advertise your services to the book trade. It will cost money to advertise in publications like *The Bookseller* and *Publishing News*, but it could be your best investment. (Remember that this is a legitimate tax-deductible expense.)

- You might think it worth advertising, too, in publications that are read by older people who might be keen to have help in writing about their lives and their travels and who are likely to have the money to pay for the job. The 'heavier' national newspapers and magazines like *The Field* and *The Lady* could reach the readership you're looking for.

- Set up your own website to advertise your service. See Chapter 12.

- If you are an expert or have at least a sound knowledge, gained from personal experience, of some business, trade or industry, try a direct mail shot to everyone you know in that line, offering your services.

- Try approaching publishers with a mail shot, offering your services as a ghostwriter. Publishers often receive proposals from would-be authors who have a potentially big-selling idea but don't have the writing skills required. If you are already published, include samples of your work. Take care to demonstrate your own writing and marketing abilities in your mail shot. No one will be interested if you send out a sloppy ill-thought-out document.

## Finding more information on ghostwriting

Google 'ghostwriting' and be amazed! Explore just a few of the 44,500 websites offered and see what other ghostwriters are doing. You'll find advice and information as well as picking up tips on how to make your own website effective. It's well worth an hour or two of your time.

The Society of Authors' *Quick Guide to Ghostwriting and Collaboration Agreements* gives advice and guidance on the subject. See under 'Further Reading'.

### Make a note

- Most writers have had this experience at some time: you're at a conference or a lecture or even a party when someone corners you and says, 'You're a writer, aren't you? Well, I've got a brilliant idea for a book. Why don't I give you the idea, you write the book, and we'll split the profits 50–50?' Say 'No thanks' and walk away. Don't even think about it. This kind of lop-sided arrangement is no basis for a partnership. And who needs someone else's idea anyway—the idea is the easiest part of any writing project. It's the hard graft of writing that turns the idea into a book.

## Points to remember

- There is always a demand for human interest stories.
- Be aware of the problems that might mar a lengthy collaboration.
- Both parties need to maintain a professional attitude throughout a collaboration—it's a mistake to get too chummy.
- Check that all agreements are drawn up to be fair to both parties.
- Check that you've safeguarded your copyright and financial interests.
- You and your collaborator must register individually for Public Lending Right.
- There is good money to be made from ghostwriting.
- Make sure that any ghostwriting contract you enter into is properly drawn up and fair to both parties.

# 12 **Promoting your book**

## Working with your publisher's publicity team

Books don't sell themselves. Everyone concerned needs to contribute whatever efforts they can towards a book's success. This includes the author. Long gone are the days when all the author had to do was write the book, sit back, and wait for the royalties to roll in.

Your publisher already knows a lot about you, from the information you supplied with your proposal and from the questionnaire you're likely to have filled in at his request.

The publicity team might not see this, though, especially if the publishing house is a large one and its departments work with degrees of separation. The publicity team might want additional information. Give them whatever they ask for—they're on your side.

Your cooperation is vital. Be ready to play a full part when they ask you to do book signings, interviews for the press, on radio, and perhaps on television. (A spot on *Richard & Judy*? You could get that lucky.)

Respond with enthusiasm, whatever you're asked to do—you're all working towards the same goal.

Meet the publicity team if you can. Person-to-person contact builds trust and helps to avoid misunderstandings. If your publisher sells through a team of sales representatives try to meet, or at least speak with, the person who covers your area. Let them know you're available for any book signings they might be able to arrange for you.

You might think up great publicity ideas yourself, but do run them past the team before you act on them. If the publicists don't like your suggestions, don't push. Respect their experience, and recognise the fact that they, not you, are responsible for publicity, for the budget, and for any decisions taken in this field.

Keep the team informed of any local activities you're taking part in. They might be able to supply display material to help you promote your book. Don't contact local papers, radio or any other means of publicity without first consulting with the team. It could be embarrassing if you and the publicist were to make separate approaches to the same people—you don't want to look like amateurs.

### Make a note

- Work with your publicity people, not against them. You both have the same objective—to sell as many copies of your book as possible.
- Always keep in mind that it's the team's responsibility, not yours, to make the best use of your book's publicity budget.

- Say 'Yes' to everything. Never turn down a chance to promote your book, even if it means getting up at some unearthly hour to get to a radio or TV station. Be brave. Don't be scared to try something you've never done before. As well as helping to sell your book, it could open doors for you in the future.

## Giving a talk

Whether you're invited to speak to a small group or a hall full of people, the key to giving a successful talk is thorough preparation.

Here are some strategies to help you make the occasion enjoyable and informative for your audience and a pleasant experience for yourself.

Plan ahead. Plan your talk and plan how you will handle the event. Here are some tips on how to do it.

### Planning the talk

1. Make a list of everything you want to say to this particular audience. Use the mind-mapping technique to help you remember everything you want to include. Look through your book, too—you might find it hard to believe, but authors sometimes forget what they've written! When you have every point you plan to cover down on paper, you can select those most appropriate to this particular group of people.

Be selective. Don't try to cover everything. You're aiming both to inform and to entertain your audience, not to impress them with your own brilliance.

The points you cover and the angle you take on them will vary for different audiences. You might be invited to speak to several groups in your area, depending on the scope of your topic's appeal. You might see the same people in the audience at more than one of your talks. You don't want to get a reputation for repeating the same old stuff everywhere you go. (This does tend to happen on the writing circuit—you see a name on the list of speakers and you know you're going to hear one out of only two or three talks which, if you've been around the business for a while, you're sure to have heard at least once already.)

### Make a note

- Be selective in the points you cover in your talk. Fit the content to the audience.

2. When you've decided which points you want to cover, list them in the running order that will best give your talk both cohesion and flow. Under each point, write in detail what you plan to say.

When you're happy with your plan, distil each point down to one or two short sentences. Get some index cards. Coloured ones work best—the colours help you remember the running order, and you're less likely to get the cards mixed up. Using one card for each main point, write your key sentences in letters clear enough and large enough to read even if you forget your reading glasses.

Number the cards in the order you've planned. You won't be reading from them, just referring to them when you need to—they're there simply as prompts so you won't leave anything out and to make sure you won't dry up.

The last step is to plan, at least approximately, how long each part of your talk will take, and a timetable (with the hours and minutes) for your talk—see under 'Plan the occasion', below.

File your detailed notes for future reference.

### Make a note

- Planning and timing your talk will take a lot of the stress out of the occasion. Knowing that you have all your main points, with their timing, on your cards will help you relax and speak with confidence.

3. Ask the organiser who contacted you to invite members of the group or society to send you questions in advance. The organiser can collect these and send them to you in a batch in plenty of time for you to prepare answers before the occasion.

Ask for each person's name to be included with their question. This tactic serves a triple purpose:

a) The questions will give you an idea of the kind of information most likely to interest this audience
b) You have a means of making immediate contact, by name, with members of the audience, and
c) You can feel confident that at least a few people are going to get what they want from your talk.

## Planning the occasion

1. Double check the arrangements with the organiser:

a) Date and time
b) Venue, and directions if you need them
c) Car parking facilities, if you need them
d) Who will meet you and where
e) The size of the venue, how many people are expected to attend, and whether there is a sound system
f) Whether you'll be expected to stand at a lectern or sit at a table. If you can't cope physically with standing for however long the event will last, make sure the organiser knows and provides a seat for you
g) Your place in the running order of the event—there might be minutes to be read or announcements to be made, or even other speakers before you. You need to know your scheduled starting time so you can plan a timetable for your talk. You also need to know the timing of any interval or break for tea. Plan your talk around this so you won't have to stop in the middle of making a point
h) Can you take copies of your books for sale? Will there be display facilities?

2. Dress appropriately:
   Ask the organiser what the usual dress code is for the event and the venue. It's important for your confidence that you feel suitably dressed. Don't wear anything too striking—you want the audience's attention to focus on what you're saying, not on what you're wearing.

**Make a note**

- Don't wear new clothes. Wear something you feel comfortable and at ease in. Your attention should be on your audience and on what you're saying, not on an uncomfortably tight collar or a wayward strap.
- Ask for a glass of water to be provided before you begin your talk.

Here's a tip from my own experience:

> When I gave my first platform talk to a gathering of writers I was, frankly, terrified. After the event I asked my husband, who had been sitting at the back of the hall, how he thought it had gone. He said, 'Absolutely fine—till you picked up that bit of paper just before you finished. I could see then how badly your hand was shaking.'

**Make a note**

- Don't pick anything up unless you're sure your hand is steady.

## Delivering the talk

1. As soon as you get on to the platform or sit down at your table, place your prompt cards where you can see them easily, and take off your wristwatch and place it, too, where you can see the time at a glance. You need to keep to your schedule without making it obvious. If you have to lift or turn your wrist to consult your watch you'll distract both yourself and your audience.

2. Make sure you can be heard. If there is no amplification system, talk to the back of the room. Speak clearly and at a slow enough pace to be sure your audience hears every word.

3. Introduce one of the questions you've been sent early in your talk. Ask the questioner to identify him- or herself: 'This question comes from Polly Pink. Where are you, Polly? Hello …' thus making direct contact with the audience. Be careful, though, not to open the door to a flood of other questions on the same topic—you'll never get to the end of your talk if you let this happen. When

you've answered Polly Pink's question, say with a smile that if anyone else wants to ask a question you'll make sure there's plenty of time at the end, but you have a lot to say before that. Filter the other prepared questions and answers in as you go along.

4. At question time, either you or the chair person should repeat the questions clearly, so that the audience can relate your answer to what has been asked. We've all been in that irritating situation where someone in the front row asks a question and no one else knows what the answer refers to. Avoid getting into a one-to-one conversation with someone at the front of the hall—this will annoy everyone else.

5. If a member of the audience disagrees with something you say, keep cool. Don't get into an argument. There are people around who make a practice of trying to stir things up. Don't let them get to you. Speak calmly, say to this person that they are, of course, entitled to their view. Smile—and move on.

6. Be prepared in case no one asks you a question. Have a few of your own roughed into your notes, so that if there is no response to 'Any more questions?' you can carry on with 'Many people are keen to know how …' You can then round up your talk in this way.

7. Be ready to spend some time with people who want to chat to you after your talk is finished. Some people are too shy to speak from the floor, so be patient and answer any questions they want to ask you in semi-privacy.

8. Above all, be positive. Whatever you're talking about, adopt a 'can do' attitude and encourage your audience to do the same. They want to hear about what they can do, not how difficult everything is. Your reason for being there is to help promote your book. A negative attitude on your part is not going to persuade them either to buy the book or to recommend it to their friends.

One particular evening at a writer's conference comes to mind every time I hear a speaker take a negative view of a subject. The scheduled speaker that evening was a top agent, and the whole place was buzzing with anticipation. We expected all kinds of encouraging tips on what publishers wanted, how we should go about the business of getting our work published and suchlike. What we got was a litany of negatives: how impossible it was to break in at this particular time, how reluctant agents were to take on new clients, how slim were the chances of success for a new writer ... on and on it went.

The pall of gloom over the hall grew ever deeper, as people contemplated whether to top themselves there and then or wait till they got back to their room. Three hundred people left that hall with their hopes and dreams in shreds.

Make it your aim to fill your audience with enthusiasm. Make them believe they can do anything they choose to do. Send them off feeling empowered and confident and they'll love both you and your book.

You could also send them off with a sheet of information that covers the main points of your talk and, of course, gives details of how they can obtain your book. You could even include an order form. It's worth a try. Everybody loves a hand-out.

### Make a note

- Send your audience home with a smile on their faces and hope in their hearts. They're far more likely to buy your book if they believe it will make them feel good about themselves, whatever your topic.

## Preparing for interviews

### Newspapers

Get as much local coverage as you can. You or your publicity team (liaise with them about this) should send review copies with your biographical and contact details to the arts correspondents of any newspapers published in your area.

A good review coupled with information about you as a local author doesn't only help sell your book but can also generate interest from groups who might invite you to speak to them. Ideally, you want as many newspapers as possible to feature a review and information about your book coupled with an interview.

We looked at interviewing techniques in Chapter 5. You learned there how to get interviewees to open up and give you the information you want. Now it's you who are going to be interviewed, and you can be sure the reporter will be armed with all these techniques and more.

You'll probably be interviewed at home. Welcome your interviewer warmly, as you would any other guest. The paper might send a photographer along at the same time, or possibly at a different time or even on a different day. Don't worry about preparing for this. The professional photographer will select a pose for you that they judge to be best for an effective but natural result.

Don't let your guard down completely during the interview, though. Be aware that your interviewer will want to include as much human interest as possible, so be a wee bit canny with your answers. Don't volunteer anything you (or yours) would not be happy to see in print. You won't be given copy approval, so anything you say could be taken down and used to spark up a feature.

If a reporter from another area reads about you and contacts you asking for an interview, don't commit yourself before you've discussed the request with your team. Get the caller's name and number and say you'll get back to them. Your team might have other contacts in that area, and could be in the process of arranging an interview with a rival publication.

### Make a note

- Keep your wits about you when you're being interviewed. Don't let a skilful reporter coax information out of you that you wouldn't be happy to see in print.
- Contact your publicity team before you agree to interviews. They might have arrangements in the pipeline that would cause a clash of interests.

## Radio

Radio people live in a different time dimension from the rest of us. Every section of every radio programme, from news broadcasts to drama, from talks to current affairs, is timed to the second. This can be disconcerting for anyone new to broadcasting. Listen closely to a few different live programmes, not just for the content but for the timing. You will seldom hear silence.

Be prepared for life on the edge. If your interview is going out live—and most do—it will either be broadcast from your nearest studio or by a telephone link from your home.

For a studio interview you should arrive in plenty of time. If you're driving to the studio, phone ahead to check the parking arrangements. If there is a car park on the premises, you'll probably have to arrange access permission in advance. Take some identification with you. Security is taken very seriously, and you'll be stopped at the gate while your identity is checked and your permission verified.

You'll then report at the reception desk, where someone will come out to meet you and show you where to wait. This is the nerve-racking bit. You'll watch one of the many clocks tick the seconds and minutes away. Don't panic. You have not been forgotten! The procedure might appear chaotic to you, but it's actually tightly organised.

What happens next depends on what kind of programme your interview will be part of, and whether you're going to be patched through to another part of the country. Put your trust in your escort—they know what they're doing.

If you're going to be interviewed at home by telephone, someone will contact you beforehand to check on the line quality and to give you the exact time you're going to be on air. Your interviewer will probably speak to you before the interview, and might tell you what form it will take. Or you might find yourself going straight on air. Again, don't panic. Let the interviewer lead you, relax, and try to enjoy the experience. It will get easier with practice.

Your might be asked to take part in a phone-in, when listeners ask questions. This can seem daunting, but be confident you'll cope—after all, you've published a book on the topic they'll be asking about. To them, you're the expert. Talk to the caller as you would talk to a friend who is interested in what you have to say.

Speak clearly, and not too quickly. The listeners are relying on your voice and your words. They have no visual aids to help them understand what you're telling them.

### Make a note

- Keep calm, and do whatever is asked of you.
- Smile while you're talking—this will help you to sound relaxed.

Don't *ever* give out your telephone number on air. You could be inviting all kinds of nuisance calls, and even people who are genuinely interested in you and in what you've written about can be selfish and inconsiderate and might call you at any time of the day or night. Simply, *don't do it.*

If you have a website, promote that by all means. Or you might think about creating an e-mail address to use exclusively for enquiries about your book. Either way, you keep control of the contacts.

Here's a tip to help you feel more relaxed about taking part: Look on the station's website for information about the person you're going to be speaking with. You'll probably find a photograph and enough biographical detail to give you a feel for the kind of person this is. Print out the information and the photograph. You'll be happier and more relaxed talking to someone whose face you can see and who you know, for example, loves gardening, has three children and is potty about cats. It puts you on a more equal footing, as this person will know a lot about you from the information your publicity team has supplied along with the review copy of your book.

## Television

The first time you're invited to go on television you're going to feel nervous. There's no point telling you not to worry—you will. But you're going to do the broadcast anyway, so maybe the following reassurances will help to calm you a little.

Arrive in plenty of time, and put yourself in the hands of the production team. They know their business and they'll do their best to put you at ease. If the programme is being made in a studio, expect some attention from a make-up artist. Trust them to know what they're doing. Man or woman, you'll look better under the bright hot lights when they've balanced your face colour and eliminated most of the inevitable shine.

The production team will be happy if you don't wear

- bright white—it can cause glare
- small patterns or stripes, especially narrow stripes—they can cause shimmer
- shiny fabrics—they can reflect light
- sparkling jewellery—it can cause flashes of light.

There might be time for the programme's presenter to have a word with you before you go on air, but if there isn't time for this just try to be as natural as you can and try not to fidget. Unless the programme format requires you to talk straight to the viewer, which is unusual, you'll be asked *not* to look at the camera. The aim will be to make your chat with the host look as natural as possible.

Take a copy of your book with you. The producer, or possibly the presenter, will have one, but don't rely on them having it in the studio. You're there to promote your book, so make sure there's a copy in view. Hold it the right way up and facing out, not flat on your lap.

You might have to wait in the 'green room', the hospitality suite, where there will be refreshments laid on. *Do not* be tempted to have an alcoholic drink 'to steady your nerves'. You need to be fully in command of yourself, so you can answer questions coherently. Remember, too, that alcohol could make you sweat under the studio lights. Abstain, please.

### Make a note

- Always have a copy of your book with you.
- Don't drink alcohol before an interview—it might show.

### Local television

With the ever widening spread of broadband and digital services, local television is likely to be as universal as local radio within a few years. Look forward to that—it will help us all sell more books.

Respond positively to any requests for interviews or talks, but consult your publicity team before committing yourself.

## Book signings

As well as signing books you sell to members of the audience when you give talks, you might be able to arrange—or have your publicity people arrange for you—signings in local bookshops. Whoever makes the arrangements, you need to be sure there will be plenty of copies of your book available in the shop.

This kind of event is unpredictable. Don't expect too much. Be delighted if you have a steady stream of book buyers queuing up for your signature, but try not to be disappointed if business is slow or even non-existent. This can happen to the most famous authors.

If you're in an independent bookshop, play fair and only sign books the customers buy or copies the owner asks you to sign. If, on the other hand, you're in a branch of one of the big chains, sign as many copies as you can—signed books can't be returned to the publisher. All's fair in love and bookselling.

## Writers' events and literary festivals

Try to go to as many events as you can. There will usually be opportunities to promote and possibly sell your book. The writers' residential events at Caerleon and Swanwick, for example, have a book room devoted to displaying and selling delegates books.

The *Writers' & Artists' Yearbook* carries a pretty comprehensive list of such events. Your local and regional newspapers should have 'events' or 'arts' columns where you can find out what's happening in your area. Don't miss any chance that presents itself—one thing can often lead to another…

## Getting reviews in print media

You'll be asked to supply the publicity team with names and addresses of publications and newsletters that would be interested in reviewing your book. The number of review copies your publisher will be prepared to send out will depend on the publicity budget allocated to your book, but give as many contacts as you can think of, beginning with the most influential at the top of the list.

If you have already had personal contact with any of your listed publications—maybe you've written articles for them or have met an editor or other member of staff at an event—give them a call beforehand to alert them that the review copy will be coming.

Each review copy will be sent out with a prepared Advance Information sheet that gives all the necessary information about your book and about yourself. Your team should make sure all the necessary contact details are complete and correct.

## Getting reviews on the internet

Internet websites with an interest in your topic will probably be delighted to feature a ready-made review. Most sites are thirsting for copy most of the time. If you have an internet-savvy friend who enjoys reviewing books, ask them to write a review and send it to as many relevant sites as possible. In return for this favour, they get to keep the book—and maybe a 'thank you' meal or a drink.

## Promoting your book on your own website

Set up a website, however basic, if you can. This need not cost a lot. Many internet service providers allocate a certain amount of web space as part of the subscription deal. Even a two- or three-page site will give you enough space to include a brief author biography, a photo of your book's cover, a synopsis, details of how and where to buy the book, and links to other relevant websites. As you gain more online experience, you can think of expanding to a more sophisticated set-up.

The important thing is to have a presence on the web and for people to be able to find your site easily. Links matter. You'll put them on your site in a mutually beneficial arrangement with other website owners with interests in your topic, however tenuous. They will return the favour, directing people to your site via links on theirs. This is how the world of web publicity turns. It costs you nothing to do someone a favour, but could reap rich rewards in the form of book sales.

### Make a note

- A web presence, however modest, is essential—and expected—for any writer nowadays.

Make your website as simple and easy to navigate as possible. The golden rule here is 'Less is more'. Read a good book on copywriting to see how to use the available space to greatest effect. In his chapter on writing for the web, in the third (2005) edition of his *The Copywriter's Handbook*, American author Robert W Bly writes, 'Ten years ago, 100 percent of my copywriting was print and zero percent was on the internet. Today, 50 percent of my copywriting is print and 50 percent is online.'

If you need basic guidance on setting up your website, consult a good book like Richard Quick's *Web Design in easy steps*. This straightforward guide cuts through the mystique and takes the fear out of the process, using plenty of colour illustrations and uncomplicated language to help you 'design websites like a pro'.

## Selling and promoting your book on Amazon

Your objective is to promote your book by every (legal) means you can. Your publisher will be selling your book through the online bookseller Amazon. If he doesn't, ask why. You can help sell copies by opening an Amazon account and signing up to sell your book through their 'Marketplace' facility.

### Make a note

- Check that the Amazon entry for your book is accurate, and includes the correct details and synopsis. Mistakes have been known to happen.

You'll be given space to include a few words promoting the merits of your book. You can fix your own price, and Amazon compensates you for postage costs by charging the buyer and passing most of the money on to you. Customise your book by offering signed first editions.

## Selling and promoting your book on eBay

Sign up as a trader with the online marketplace eBay. You can offer signed first editions of your book to other eBay users all over the world. It costs nothing to join.

Invest a fiver in *The Beginner's Guide to Buying and Selling on eBay* by Clare McCann. This pocket-size book will tell you all you need to know about simple online trading just as effectively as bigger and more expensive manuals.

## Blogging

If you enjoy writing about your book and its topic, think about starting a blog. This is an online diary or 'weblog' that can be found and read by anyone interested in you or your topic. Your ISP probably offers a blog facility you could join, or you could make your blog part of your website.

If you start a blog, though, you should be prepared to spend time regularly keeping it up to date. Many a blogger who starts with great gusto finds the exercise soon becomes a bore, and gives it up.

## Podcasting

A podcast is an online broadcast. Podcasting allows anyone with a computer, an internet connection and a microphone to broadcast to audiences all over the world. The podcast can be downloaded to portable media players, so it can be listened to at any time.

For you, as an author, podcasting gives you an additional way to reach potential buyers by talking about your topic and your book to anyone who cares to tune in and pick up your broadcast. Your podcast could either be a one-off or a series.

Podcasting is free, and is quickly becoming a favoured method of communication. Find out more by logging on to Wikipedia.

## Points to remember

- It's in your own best interests to work in harmony with your publisher's publicity people.
- When you're invited to talk about your book, take time to prepare your talk well in advance and to tailor its content to the interests of your audience.
- Prepare well, too, for interviews, and keep calm.
- When giving interviews in to any of the media, be cautious about revealing personal information.
- Never give out your phone number in interviews.
- Go to as many writers' and literary events as you can.
- Use the internet in every way possible to help promote your book.
- Get your book out there where people who need it can find it.

A final word…

Now you have all the information you need to set out on your how-to writing career. You know you can do it.

I wish you all the joy and luck in the world, and I look forward to hearing about your success.

# Glossary of terms

## How to speak 'Publishing'

Publishing people tend to talk in jargon. You'll feel more confident and more professional if you understand the language commonly used in the business. Here are simple definitions of terms frequently used by editors and publishers, focusing on non-fiction writing. For a comprehensive list of terms used over all branches of publishing, I recommend *The Guardian Dictionary of Publishing and Printing* (A & C Black).

Advance. Money paid to an author in advance of publication of his or her book, often paid in two or three parts. Under the usual terms the publisher will retain the author's royalty until the advance is paid off, after which the author receives his agreed share of the profits.

Advance Information sheet (AI). Publicity document giving sales and marketing information issued by a publisher before publication of a book.

Advertorial. Article on a company or product used as an advertisement; the words 'advertising feature' usually appear at the top of the page.

Agent. Person who negotiates between writer and publisher, for a fee.

Agreement. See Contract.

Air. The white space on a printed page.

Angle. Treatment of a topic to serve a particular purpose and influence the reader's response.

Appendix (pl. appendices). Section at the end of a book giving supplementary information.

Article. A piece of journalistic writing.

Artwork. Illustrations, photographs, ornamental lettering, fancy headings etc, pretty much anything that isn't part of the text.

**Assignment.** Request to a freelance from an editor to produce material on a specific topic; wordage, angle, fee and possibly a kill fee are usually agreed in advance.

**Author biography/bio.** Information about an author, including previously published works, often included in an Advance Information sheet.

**Author questionnaire.** Form sent to an author requesting details about his life, for publicity purposes, and for ideas on marketing his book.

**Author's alterations/author's corrections.** Changes to proofs made by an author additional to corrections of typos etc. Might be charged to the author if excessive.

**Author's proofs.** Proof copy sent to the author for reading and correction.

**B&W.** Abbreviation for 'black and white', with reference to photographs.

**Backlist.** Titles released earlier by a publisher that continue to sell.

**Back matter.** Material printed at the end of a book, after the main text: appendices, reference material, index and so on.

**Blog.** A web log = an online diary.

**Blurb.** Short promotional text on a book jacket/cover or on publicity material.

**Breakeven point.** The point at which sales of a book cover its production costs but don't yet show a profit.

**Broadband.** Continuously open connection allowing internet, telephone and fax to be used at the same time.

**Bullet/bullet point.** Large dot preceding and emphasising an item in a book or article, often used in lists.

**Byline.** Line before or after a piece of writing, identifying the writer.

**©.** Symbol signifying that a work is protected by copyright.

**Camera-ready.** Describing material ready to be photographed or scanned for printing.

**Caption.** Descriptive note above, below or beside a cartoon, illustration or photograph.

**Catchline.** Identification line at the top of a page of typescript or of a proof, discarded when the work is printed.

**Circulation.** Total number of copies distributed.

Clause. Section of a contract.

Clean copy. Manuscript or other text that is easy to read and error-free.

Clean proof. Proof needing no corrections.

Clip. Item of published work cut or photocopied from a publication. (Also called a cutting.)

Collaboration. Two or more people working together to produce a literary or artistic work, sometimes published under a single pseudonym.

Column. 1. Vertical section of writing on a page. 2. Regular section in a publication written by the same person on the same subject or a related series of subjects.

Commissioned article/commissioned book. Article or book written to the order of an editor or publisher who promises to buy the finished work on agreed terms.

Commissioning editor. Editor whose job is to commission authors to write books.

Consumer magazine. Publication covering general affairs, sports, hobbies etc. rather than business, trade or professional matter.

Contents page. Page at the beginning of a book listing, in order, everything it contains.

Contract. Signed document, an agreement between publisher and author specifying the exact responsibilities each party undertakes in the writing, production and marketing of a book, in terms of payment, assignation of rights, timetable of writing and publishing etc.

Contributing editor. Someone who contributes material regularly to a magazine but who is not a member of staff.

Contributor's copy. Copy of the issue of a magazine in which the contributor's work appears. See also 'Voucher copy'.

Copy. Term used throughout publishing for matter which is to be typeset.

Copy date. Date by which a piece of work has to be delivered to the editor.

Copy-editing. Preparation of a typescript for the printer by a specialist editor, either a member of staff or a freelance, appointed by the publisher to check facts, spelling and punctuation, syntax etc and possibly to rewrite clumsily written or inaccurate text, and to make changes to conform to house style where necessary.

Copyright. Exclusive right in his own work of an author or other designated party, as defined by law.

Copywriting. Writing material for use in advertisements, publicity, promotions etc.

Correspondent. Usually a freelance who covers a specified geographical area. Also called a stringer.

Course book. Book used by teachers and students in teaching a course.

Cover copy. See 'Blurb'.

Cover letter. Letter or e-mail sent to an agent, editor or publisher along with a proposal or manuscript or other material, giving the writer's contact details and any other necessary information.

Cover mount. Free gift attached to the cover of a magazine.

Craft book. Book dealing with practical work done by hand, e.g., sewing, collage, jewellery-making, pottery, painting etc.

Critique. Critical examination and written assessment of a work.

Crop. To cut off part(s) of an illustration.

Current list. Publisher's list of titles currently available.

CV = Curriculum vitae. Listing of qualifications and achievements.

Deadline. Latest date or time by which a job must be finished.

Defamation. Damage to someone's name or reputation. See also Libel.

Department. Ongoing section of a magazine.

Desktop. The computer screen, where icons for programs etc are shown.

Draft. Preliminary version.

DTP (desktop publishing). Computer programs for designing pages (text and pictures) on-screen instead of pasting up on paper.

Earned out. Term applied when a book has earned royalties equal to the advance paid to its author.

E-book (electronic book). Book stored on computer file and readable on-screen rather than on paper.

Edition. One printing of a book. A second or subsequent edition will have alterations, sometimes substantial, compared with previous edition(s).

Editorial. 1. Introductory column in a magazine or newspaper, usually written by the editor. 2. Text other than advertising copy.

Editorial policy. The editor's concept of the kind of publication he wants to produce.

Electronic submission. Submission made by e-mail or on a computer disk.

E-mail. Electronic mail, sent via the internet.

E-zine. Magazine created and read on-screen.

Fact. A reality as distinct from an idea or belief.

Faction. Writing which blurs the distinction between fact and fiction.

FAQ(s). Frequently asked question(s).

FBSR (First British Serial Rights). The right to publish an article or story for the first time, and once only, in the UK. (Not used when referring to books.)

Feature. Magazine or newspaper article that is not one of a series. Usually refers to a human interest piece as distinct from a news item.

Fiction. Writing that is not and does not pretend to be truth but is entirely drawn from the imagination.

Filler. Short material used to fill a column when the text doesn't fill it completely. Can be applied to any short piece.

Folio. 1. A leaf, ie, two pages of a book back to back on a single sheet of paper. 2. A page number. 3. A manuscript page.

Font (also fount). A specific design of typeface.

Foreign rights. Rights for work published in other languages for sale abroad.

Format. Size, shape and general layout.

'Freebie'. A slang term for a publication distributed free to travellers, householders etc. Anything given without charge.

Freelance. Self-employed person who sells his or her services or written work to a publisher for an agreed fee, ie, a writer/journalist selling work to various publications but not employed by any one publisher. (Derives from the mercenary knights and soldiers who wandered Europe after the Crusades, hiring out their services and their lances.)

Frontlist. A publisher's list of books new to the current season.

Ghosting/ghostwriting. Writing a book in conjunction with someone as if it had been written by the other person, often with no credit given to the writer.

Gift book. Book designed for the gift market. Often in a small format and written to fit a particular niche—for mothers, fathers, grandfathers, cat- and dog-lovers, gardeners, golfers etc, commonly displayed near tills and check-outs to tempt the impulse buyer.

Glossy. Magazine printed on heavy shiny paper rather than plain paper.

Gsm. Grammes per square metre. Refers to the weight of paper.

Guidelines/writers' guidelines. Detailed specification of a publication's editorial requirements, terms etc.

Hack. Derogatory term for someone who writes primarily for money.

Hardback. Book bound in boards rather than paper or card. Also called 'hardcover'.

Hard copy. Print-out on paper of material held on computer.

Honorarium. Small token payment.

Hook. Strong beginning designed to grab and hold the reader's attention.

House. Jargon for 'publishing company'.

House magazine. Magazine produced by a company for its employees.

House style. Consistent style in which a publisher's books or magazines are produced.

Human interest. Material about people, their achievements, problems, ambitions, social and economic circumstances etc.

Imprint. The printer's name, with the place and time of printing, required by law in many countries to be shown on published material. 2. The name of the publisher with the place and date of publication.

Indemnity. See Warranty.

In-house. Work done or ideas generated by a publisher or publication's own staff.

Internet. Global collection of computer networks with a common addressing scheme.

Intro (Abbreviation of 'Introduction'). Opening paragraph of a feature or article, possibly printed in bigger and/or bolder type than the body of the piece.

IRC (International Reply Coupon). Voucher sold at post offices worldwide, equivalent to the minimum postal rate for a letter from the country from which the letter is to be sent.

ISBN (International Standard Book Number). Unique reference number allocated to every book published, to identify its area of origin, publisher and title.

ISP (Internet Service Provider). Intermediary between the internet and the user.

ISSN (International Standard Series Number). Reference number given to periodical publications in a system similar to the ISBN.

Journalist. Person who writes for a journal, newspaper, periodical and the like.

Justified setting/justification. Spacing out of words so that each line of text is the same length, flush left and right.

Juvenile. Term commonly used for children's books.

Kill fee. Fee paid to a writer when, through no fault of theirs, a commissioned piece is not used.

Landscape. Page that is wider than it is high. Compare with 'portrait'.

Layout. Overall appearance of a script or a printed page.

Lead. Journalistic term referring to the opening of a news story or magazine article.

Lead time. Time between the copy date and the date of publication.

Leader. Principal piece in a newspaper or magazine, a main story or article.

Leading. The white space between lines of type (goes back to the days when type was set in hot metal, ie, lead).

Libel. A statement written, printed or broadcast in any medium which defames an identifiable living person by holding them up to hatred, ridicule or contempt.

Line art. Line drawings, eg, cartoons, diagrams.

List. Books that a publisher has in print.

Literary agent. Person who acts on behalf of authors in their dealings with publishers, placing their work and negotiating contracts.

Little magazine. Small circulation magazine.

Manuscript (abbreviation ms). Typewritten or word-processed text.

Market study. Analytical study of possible points of sale.

Mass market paperbacks. Paperbacks cheaply printed in large quantities.

Masthead. List of people who work on a magazine, with their work titles.

Matter. Term applied to a manuscript or other copy to be printed.

Media. Information sources: newspapers, magazines, radio, television, internet news services and so on. (Plural of medium, ie, 'medium of communication'.)

Midlist. Book that sells reasonably well but doesn't make the bestseller list. Also applied to authors of such books.

Modem. Device connecting a computer to a telephone line.

Moral right. Introduced in the Copyright, Designs and Patents Act of 1988, Moral Right complements but does not supersede copyright. It gives the writer the right to be identified as the author of his or her own work and prevents anyone else from distorting or mutilating that work. However, unlike in the rest of Europe, where Moral Right is undisputed and automatic, in the UK it must be asserted in writing, otherwise it is deemed not to exist.

Ms. Abbreviation of Manuscript.

Multiple submissions. The same material submitted to more than one editor at a time.

Net royalty. Royalty based on the actual amount of money the publisher receives after discounts and returns.

Nostalgia. Genre (usually sentimental) recalling events and/or products of the past.

'On spec'/on speculation. Applied to writing submitted to an editor on a speculative basis, ie, not invited or commissioned. Also applied to work sent at an editor's invitation but without any commitment on the editor's part.

Option. Right granted by an author to a publisher entitling them to the first chance to acquire that author's next book.

Out of print. No longer on the publisher's list, ie, no longer available except possibly from libraries or second-hand book dealers.

Outline. Sketched-out structure showing what an article or book will contain, but with little detail.

Outright payment/outright sale. One-off payment where the publisher buys all rights from the author.

'Over the transom'. American slang for the arrival of unsolicited work.

Overview. First part of a book proposal, describing the book and its potential market.

PA. Personal assistant.

Packager. Company that takes the concept of a book to a publisher and then oversees the creation of the project by writers, designers etc; the resulting product is then released by the publisher.

Page rate. Fixed or agreed rate per published page rather than payment by wordage.

Para. Shorthand for 'paragraph'.

Payment on acceptance. The writer's dream scenario, all too rare nowadays: the editor pays for your work as soon as he accepts it for publication.

Pen name. A name other than your own that you use on articles and books. See also Pseudonym.

Photo feature. Feature where the pictures are more important and prominent than the words.

Pic/pix. Jargon for 'picture/pictures'.

Picture agency. Organisation storing photographs and/or illustrations and leasing reproduction rights.

Picture fees. Fees paid for the right to reproduce photographs and/or illustrations in which the user does not hold the copyright.

Piece. Jargon for any short piece of writing, whether article or feature.

Plagiarism. The use without permission, whether deliberate or accidental, of work in which the copyright is held by someone other than the user.

PLR (Public Lending Right). System of monetary reward for writers, based on the number of times their works are borrowed from public libraries.

Portrait. A page that is higher than it is wide. Compare with 'landscape'.

Prelims (preliminary pages). Opening pages of a book: title page, publishing history, contents and so on.

Print on demand. An electronic process for printing books to order.

Professional journal. Publication produced specifically for circulation in a particular profession, eg, *The Lancet* (medicine).

Program. Universally accepted spelling of 'programme' when related to computing.

Proof. An impression of typeset matter for checking and correction before the final printing.

Proposal. Summary of an idea for a book, particularly applied to non-fiction, usually put to the publisher as an initial query, then as a sales package including a synopsis of the whole work with a sample chapter or two.

Pseudonym. A fictitious name used by an author. See 'pen name'.

Public domain. Material that has either never been in copyright or is now out of copyright is referred to as being 'in the public domain'.

Publication date. Date when a book is delivered to retailers.

Publisher's reader. Person employed to evaluate a manuscript and to supply a written summary and report, to help the publisher assess its potential as a published work.

Pull quote. Quotation extracted from an article and printed in a prominent position on the page.

Q&A/Question and Answer. Interview or other piece in the form of a series of questions and answers.

Query. Enquiry, by letter or e-mail, from a writer to an editor asking if he or she would be interested in seeing a piece of the writer's work.

Reader profile. The perceived average reader of a specific publication, assessed in terms of age range, social status, financial status/spending power, educational level and leisure interests.

Readership. Collective term applied to the people who regularly read a particular publication.

Recto page. The right-hand page of an open book.

Remainders. Unsold books offered by the publisher to specialist dealers for a small percentage of the cover price.

Reprint rights. Right to republish a book, either in its original format or in a different format or version after first publication.

Reserve. Funds not paid out to the author but reserved against the publisher's estimation of books that might be returned by booksellers.

Returns. Unsold books sent back to the publisher from bookshops and distributors, for credit.

Review copies. Free copies sent before publication to book reviewers and other possible sources of publicity.

Rights. Those parts of an author's copyright which he leases to a publisher as specified in a contract.

Round-up article. Article containing interviews with or comments from a number of people relating to a specific topic.

RoW = rest of the world. Anywhere outside a specified geographic area.

Royalty. Percentage of either the cover price or the net receipts of a book payable to the author under the terms of a contract after any advance has been recovered.

Royalty-free copies. Books sent out for review or given away for publicity purposes, complimentary copies given to the author under the terms of the contract, or books returned from bookshops or wholesalers.

Running headlines. The headings that run across the top of the pages, usually incorporating the page numbers. Also called 'Running heads'.

Saddle-stitched. Stapled through the back centre fold.

Sae/stamped self-addressed envelope. Envelope addressed back to the sender, bearing adequate postage stamps or sent with adequate IRCs. (US: Sase.)

Scanning. Process by which high quality printed text and photographs are read by a computer scanner and converted into usable data.

'Scissors-and-paste job'. Contemptuous term applied to work that consists of material 'lifted' from reference books, encyclopaedias, magazines and so on, rearranged and then passed off as an original piece of writing.

Search engine. Electronic 'catalogue' capable of storing and finding hundreds of millions of website addresses and able to search out pages of material relevant to a user's request.

Self-publishing. A venture in which an author publishes his own book rather than offering it to a traditional publishing company. See also 'Vanity publishing'.

Serial rights. Rights covering material sold to magazines and newspapers. (Does not necessarily mean that the material will be printed in instalments.)

Setting. The process of turning typewritten or word-processed material into type ready for printing.

Shout line. A prominent line of text on a magazine cover drawing attention to an item featured inside.

Sidebar. Short feature accompanying a news story or article, enlarging on some aspect of the piece. Usually boxed or set in a different typeface or otherwise distinguished from the main text.

Simultaneous submissions. The same material sent to more than one market at a time.

Slant. Style or approach taken to make a piece appeal to or to influence the response of a particular readership.

Slush pile. Derogatory term applied to the unsolicited mss that accumulate in an editorial office. (So called because the biggest proportion of uninvited material is romantic fiction.)

Small presses. Small businesses, often one-person operations, producing publications ranging from duplicated pamphlets to bound books, of variable quality.

Snail mail. Normal postal services as distinct from electronic mail.

Source list. A list of the people interviewed and reference works drawn on in compiling a work. (Used by fact checkers to verify information in an article.)

Spam. Uninvited and unwanted e-mail.

Spread. Matter or illustrative material set over two facing pages in a magazine.

Stable. Group of writers whose work is regularly commissioned and published by a particular magazine although they are not on its staff.

Staff writer (US: staffer). Writer employed and salaried by a publisher as distinct from a freelance.

Standfirst. Introductory paragraph in bigger and/or bolder type leading into and possibly summarising the content of an article.

Stet (Latin). An editorial instruction meaning 'let it stand'.

Story. Jargon for a feature or article. (Not to be confused with fiction stories.)

Strapline/strap. Identification line at the top of a manuscript page. See also Catchline.

Style. The way in which something is written, eg, short or long sentences and paragraphs, simple or complex language etc. See also House style.

Submission. Manuscript that is sent to a publisher with a view to publication.

Subsidiary rights. Term usually applied to rights other than UK book rights, eg, film and TV rights, foreign language rights, serial rights, electronic rights and so on.

Subsidy publisher. Another term for 'Vanity publisher'.

Syndication. The selling of the same piece several times over to non-competing publications, possibly in different countries.

Synopsis. Précis or condensed version of the theme and contents of a book, giving a clear outline of the proposed text.

Taboos. Subjects, words, references not acceptable to certain publications.

Tearsheet. Page torn from a magazine. Often used as an example of a writer's work when seeking assignments.

Technical writing. The writing of company and product manuals, reports, engineering and computing manuals and the like.

Text. The body of typeset matter in a book, as distinct from headings, footnotes, illustrations etc.

Textbook. Book created for and sold to the education market.

TOC. Table of contents.

Trade books. Books sold through traditional outlets to bookshops and book clubs.

Trade magazine. Publication produced for circulation among practitioners and companies in a particular trade or industry, eg., *The Grocer.*

Translation rights. The right to publish a book in a language other than the original language in which it was published.

Transparency. Colour photograph on slide film rather than in negative or digital form.

Unagented. Term applied to an author or book not represented by a literary agent.

Unsolicited submission. Work sent to an editor or publisher without invitation.

URL (Uniform Resource Locator). Address identifying an internet document's type and location.

Usual terms/usual rates. Usual rates of payment offered by a publication to freelance writers.

'Vanity' publishing. Term applied to the publication of work on behalf of an author who pays someone to publish the work for him.

Verso page. The left-hand page of an open book.

Viewpoint. Point of view from which a story or article is told; the selected position of the author.

Voucher copy. Copy of one issue of a publication sent free to a writer whose work appears in that issue, as a courtesy and as evidence (to vouch) that the work has in fact been published.

Warranty. The promise from author to publisher that the material supplied is original, does not infringe copyright, does not include anything potentially harmful, and will not lay the publisher open to claims of libel or damage. (Also called an Indemnity.)

Web. See World Wide Web.

Web log. See Blog.

Website. Internet location set up by individuals or companies to promote themselves, their works and their services.

Word processing program. Program using computer logic to accept, store and retrieve material for editing and printing out on paper or storing on the computer's hard disk or on removable computer software (CDs, floppy disks etc).

World Wide Web. (Also referred to as WWW or 'the web'). Network of graphic and text document 'pages' linked together electronically on the internet.

Young Adult. Term applied to books for the teenage market.

# List of topics

## How to use the list of topics

I've included this list to stimulate your imagination, and as a fall-back if you find you're running out of ideas. These are topic headings only. A list of every possible variation of every available topic would need a book on its own. Choose your topic and use the brain-storming technique shown in Chapter 1 to explore its potential. You'll never be stuck for ideas.

Remember, you don't have to know a lot about every topic that sparks your interest—you just need to know someone who does.

- Acting
- Alternative therapies
- Animal care
- Antiques
- Art, Appreciation
- Art, Practical
- Astrology
- Astronomy
- Audio
- Aviation
- Beauty
- Bee-keeping
- Bible study
- Biology
- Bird-keeping
- Bird-watching
- Birthdays
- Blindness
- Book-collecting
- Book-publishing
- Book-reading
- Book-writing
- Botany
- Broadcasting
- Building
- Business and Commerce
- Calligraphy
- Careers and Employment
- Cars and Motoring
- Cartoons
- Cats
- Ceramics
- Charity
- Chemistry
- Children
- Christmas
- Cinema
- Collecting
- Computing
- Conservation
- Cookery
- Countryside
- Crafts
- Creative writing
- Cricket
- Crime

- Culture
- Dance
- Decorative arts
- Dentistry
- Design
- Disability
- DIY
- Dogs
- Drama
- Easter
- Ecology
- Economics
- Education
- Electronics
- Emotional well-being
- Energy
- Engineering
- English language teaching
- Entertainment
- Environment
- Equal opportunities
- Etiquette and manners
- Family
- Fashion and costume
- Father's Day
- Feminism
- Festivals
- Film
- Finance
- Firearms
- Fish-keeping
- Fishing
- Fitness
- Folklore
- Food and drink
- Football
- Fortune-telling
- Franchising
- Freelancing
- Games
- Gardening
- Genealogy
- Geography
- Geology
- Golf
- 'Green' living
- Guidebooks
- Guiding
- Hallowe'en
- Health
- Heritage
- History
- Holidays
- Home-making
- Homeopathy
- Horses
- Horticulture
- Housing
- Human rights
- Humour
- Hypnotism
- Illustration
- Income tax
- Indexing
- Industrial relations
- Inheritance tax
- Interior design
- Journalism
- Language
- Law
- Leisure and Hobbies
- Libraries
- Linguistics
- Literature
- Local government
- Local interest
- Magic
- Maps

- Maritime
- Marketing
- Mathematics
- Media
- Medical matters
- Men
- Military
- Mineralogy
- Money
- Mother's Day
- Mountaineering
- Music
- Mythology
- Nature
- New Age
- New Year
- Nursing
- Occult
- Organic living
- Outdoor pursuits
- Palaeontology
- Pantomime
- Parenting
- Pets
- Philosophy
- Photography
- Phrenology
- Physics
- Poetry
- Politics
- Psychology
- Puzzles
- Radio
- Railways

- Religion
- Research
- Safety
- Savings
- Science
- Scouting
- Sex
- Show business
- Sociology
- Space and Cosmology
- Sport
- Taxation
- Technical writing
- Technology
- Teenagers
- Telecommunications
- Television
- Textbooks
- Textiles
- Theatre
- Theology
- Third Age
- Tradition
- Transport
- Travel
- Valentine's Day
- Vegetarianism
- Video
- Voluntary sector
- Wildlife
- Wine and spirits
- Woodwork
- Zoology

# Further reading

## Recommended books

*Beginner's Guide to Getting Published, The*, Chriss McCallum (How To Books, 2008).

*Copywriter's Handbook, The*, Robert W Bly (Owl Books, Henry Holt and Company LLC, 2005).

*Freelance Photographer's Market Handbook, The* (annually, The Bureau of Freelance Photographers).

*Freelance Writer's Handbook, The*, Andrew Crofts (Piatkus, 3rd edn 2002).

*From Pitch to Publication*, Carole Blake (Macmillan, 1999).

*Get Everything Done and Still Have Time to Play*, Mark Forster (Hodder & Stoughton 'Help Yourself', 2000).

*Guardian Dictionary of Publishing and Printing, The* (third edition, A&C Black, 2006).

*How to Publish Your Own Book*, Vernon Coleman (Blue Books, 1998).

*How to Write & Sell a Book Proposal*, Stella Whitelaw (Writer's Bookshop, 2000).

*How to Write & Sell a Synopsis*, Stella Whitelaw (Allison & Busby, 1993).

*How to Write Five-Minute Features—A practical guide on writing fillers, letters and other shorts*, Alison Chisholm, (Allison & Busby, 1995).

*How to Write Short-Short Stories—A practical guide on how to write—and sell—the one-page story*, Stella Whitelaw (Allison & Busby, 1996).

*Oxford Dictionary for Writers & Editors, The*, Ed R M Ritter (Oxford University Press, 2nd edn, 2000).

*60 Ways to Feel Amazing*, Lynda Field (Vermilion, 1998).

*Successful Non-Fiction Writing*, Nicholas Corder (The Crowood Press, 2006).

*Touch Typing in Ten Hours*, Ann Dobson (How To Books Ltd, 2nd revised edn 2007).

*Web Design in Easy Steps*, Richard Quick (In Easy Steps, Computer Step, 2007).

*Writer's Handbook, The*, (Macmillan, annually).

*Writer's Digest Handbook of Magazine Article Writing*, Ed Michelle Ruberg (Writer's Digest Books, 2nd edn, 2005).

*Writer's Digest* magazine (Writer's Digest Books, monthly).

*Writer's Market* (Writer's Digest Books, annually).

*Writers' & Artists' Yearbook, The*, (A&C Black, annually).

*Writing TV Scripts—Successful Writing in 10 Weeks*, Steve Wetton (Studymates, 2006).

## Other books mentioned in the text

*Age-Proof Your Brain: Sharpen Your Memory in 7 Days*, Tony Buzan (Harper Thorson's).

*Amo, Amas, Amat … and All That: How to Become a Latin Lover*, Harry Mount (Short Books, 2006).

*Beginner's Guide to Buying and Selling on eBay, The*, Clare McCann (Summersdale, 2006).

*Boys' Book, The—How to be the Best at Everything*, Guy Macdonald (Buster Books, 2006).

*Cat's Little Instruction Book, A*, Leigh W Rutledge (Thorsons, 1993).

*Children's Healthy & Fun Cookbook*, Nicola Graimes (Dorling Kindersley, 2007).

*Dangerous Book for Boys, The*, Conn and Hal Igguden (HarperCollins, 2006).

*Devil's Guide to Hollywood, The*, Joe Eszterhas (Duckworth, 2007).

*Dinner in a Dash—50 Dinners for 6 in 60 Minutes*, Lindsey Bareham (Quadrille, 2007).

*Eats, Shoots & Leaves*, Lynne Truss (Profile Books, 2003).

*Essence of Happiness: A Guidebook for Living, The*, The Dalai Lama (Hodder & Stoughton).

*Girls' Book, The—How to be the Best at Everything*, Juliana Foster (Buster Books, 2006).

*Green Self-Build Book, The—How to Enjoy Designing and Building your own Eco-home*, Jon Broome (Green Books, 2007).

*Hot Tips for the Reluctant Housewife*, Shelagh Nugent (Nightingale Press, 2001).

*House Proud—Hip Craft for the Modern Housemaker*, Danielle Proud (Bloomsbury, 2006).

*How to Be a Gardener—secrets of success*, Alan Titchmarsh (BBC Books, 2003).

*How to See Yourself as You Really Are*, The Dalai Lama (Rider).

*How to Win Friends and Influence People*, Dale Carnegie.

*I Love Knitting*, Rachel Henderson (Kyle Cathie, 2006).

*Knit 2 Together: Patterns and Stories for Serious Knitting Fun*, Tracey Ullman (Stewart, Tabori & Chang, 2006).

*Living with the Black Dog*, Caroline Carr (White Ladder, 2007).

*Mrs Beeton's Book of Household Management* (Oxford's World Classics, 2000).

*New Spend Less Revolution, The—365 Tips for a Better Quality of Life While Actually Spending Less*, Rebecca Ash (Harriman House, 2006).

*People Watching—How to Take Control*, Vernon Coleman (Blue Books, 1995).

*Peter Paints a Picture*, Saviour Pirotta and Linzi West (Frances Lincoln, 2007).

*Practical Picture-Framing Handbook, The*, Rian Kanduth (Southwater, 2006).

*Start Mosaic*, Teresa Mills (Apple Press, 2007).

*Super Brain: 101 Ways to a More Agile Mind*, Carol Vorderman (Vermilion).

*Tactics: The Art and Science of Success*, Edward de Bono (Profile, 2007).

*Upping Sticks—How to Move House and Stay Sane*, Dr Sandi Mann and Dr Paul Seager (White Ladder, 2007).

*Yes I Can! Help save our planet*, Emma Brownjohn (Tango Books, 2007).

*You Can Be Amazing: Transform Your Life With Hypnosis*, Ursula James (Century, 2007).

*You Can Stop Smoking*, Jennifer Percival (Virgin Books, 2007).

*You Didn't Hear It From Us—New York's Hippest Bartenders Tell You How to Get Your Man*, Dushan Zaric and Jason Kasmas, (Element Original).

*You Don't Need a Title to be a Leader: How Anyone, Anywhere, Can Make a Positive Difference,* Mark Sanborn, (Random House Business Books).

*Young Gardener, The,* Stefan T Buksacki (Frances Lincoln, 2006).

# Recommended publications

*Author, The* (the magazine of the Society of Authors), 84 Drayton Gardens, London SW10 9SB. Tel: 020 7373 6642. E-mail: info@societyofauthors.org www.societyofauthors. org

*Book & Magazine Collector,* Diamond Publishing Ltd, Unit 101, 140 Wales Farm Road, London W3 6UG. Tel: 0870 732 8080.

*Bookseller, The,* VNU Business Publications, 189 Shaftesbury Avenue, London WC2H 8TJ. Tel: 020 7420 6006.

*Ghostwriting and Collaboration Agreements, Quick Guide to,* The Society of Authors.

*Income Tax, Quick Guide to,* The Society of Authors.

*New Writer, The,* PO Box 60, Cranbrook, Kent TN17 2ZR. Tel: 01580 212626. E-mail: admin@thenewwriter.com

*Press Gazette,* Wilmington Media Ltd, 6–14 Underwood St, London N1 7JQ. Tel: 020 7490 0049.

*Publishing News,* 7 John Street, London WC1N 2ES. Tel: 0970 870 2345.

*Self-Publishing, Quick Guide to,* the Society of Authors.

*Writer's Digest,* Editorial Office, 4700 E. Galbraith Road, Cincinnati, Ohio OH 45236. www.writersdigest.com

*Writers' Forum* (available from W H Smith), Select Publishing Services Ltd, PO Box 6337, Bournemouth BH1 9EH. www.writers-forum.co.uk

*Writers' News,* Warners Group Publications, 5th Floor, 31–32 Park Row, Leeds, West Yorkshire LS1 5JD. Tel: 0113 200 2929. www.writersnews.co.uk

*Writing Magazine* (available from W H Smith), (address and phone number as for *Writers News*). www.writingmagazine. co.uk

## Other publications mentioned in the text

*Artist, The*, Caxton House, 63/65 High Street, Tenterden, Kent TN30 6BD. Tel: 01580 763673. Website: www. theartistmagazine.co.uk

*Car Mechanics*, Cudham Tithe Barn, Berrys Hill, Cudham, Kent TN16 3AG. E-mail: info@kelsey.co.uk

*Chat*, IPC Connect Ltd, King's Reach Tower, Stamford Street, London SE1 9LS. Tel: 020 7261 6565. Website: www.ipcmedia.com

*Country Life*, IPC Media Ltd, King's Reach Tower, Stamford Street, London SE1 9LS. www.countrylife.co.uk

*Cumbria Magazine*, Country Publications Ltd, The Water Mill, Broughton Hall, Skipton, North Yorkshire BD23 3AG. Tel: 01756 701381. E-mail: editorial@dalesman. co.uk

*Daily Telegraph, The*, 1 Canada Square, Canary Wharf, London E14 5DT. Tel: 020 7538 5000. www.telegraph. co.uk

*Devon Life*, Archant Life South, Archant Road, Babbage Road, Totnes, Devon TQ9 5JA. Tel: 01803 860910. E-mail: devonlife@archant.co.uk www.devonlife.co.uk

*Disability Now* (published by Scope), 6 Market Road, London N7 9PW. Tel: 020 7619 7323. E-mail: editor@ disabilitynow.org.uk www.disabilitynow.org.uk

*Dorset Life*, 7 The Leanne, Sandford Lane, Wareham, Dorset BH20 4DY. Tel: 01929 551264. E-mail: office@dorsetlife. co.uk

*English Garden, The*, Archant Publishing Ltd, Jubilee House, 2 Jubilee Place, London SW3 3TQ. Tel: 020 7751 4800. E-mail: theenglishgarden@archant.co.uk

*Field, The*, IPC Media Ltd, King's Reach Tower, Stamford Street, London SE1 9LS. Tel: 020 7261 5198. www.thefield. co.uk

*First News* (weekly newspaper for children), Newsbridge Limited, 12 Plumtree Court, London EC4A 4HT. Tel: 01483 281 005. Website: www.firstnews.co.uk

*Fishing News*, 4th Floor, Albert House, 1–4 Singer Street, London EC2A 4BQ. Tel: 020 7071 4531. E-mail: tim. oliver@informa.com

*Good Housekeeping*, National Magazine House, 72 Broadwick Street, London W1F 9EP. Tel: 020 7439 5000. www.natmags. co.uk

*Grocer, The*, William Reed Publishing Ltd, Broadfield Park, Crawley, West Sussex RH11 9RT. Tel: 01293 613400. www. thegrocer.co.uk

*Guardian, The*, 119 Farringdon Road, London EC1R 3ER. Tel: 020 7278 2332. www.guardian.co.uk

*Independent, The*, Independent House, 191 Marsh Wall, London E14 9RS. Tel: 020 7005 2000. www.independent. co.uk

*Ireland's Own*, Channing House, Upper Row Street, Wexford, Republic of Ireland. Tel 053 91 40140. E-mail: irelands. own@peoplenews.ie

*Justice of the Peace*, LexisNexis Butterworths, 35 Chancery Lane, London WC2A 1EL. Tel: 020 7400 2828. E-mail: jpn@lexisnexis.co.uk

*Lady, The*, 39–40 Bedford Street, London WC2E 9ER. Tel: 020 7379 4717. www.lady.co.uk

*Lancet, The*, 32 Jamestown Road, London NW1 7BY. Tel: 020 7424 4910. www.thelancet.com

*Legal Week*, Global Professional Media Ltd, 28–29 Haymarket, London SW1Y 4RX. Tel: 020 7484 9700. www.legalweek. com

*People, The* (formerly *Sunday People*), 1 Canada Square, Canary Wharf, London E14 5AP. Tel: 020 7293 3000. Website: www.people.co.uk

*Psychologies*, Hachette Filipacchi (UK) Ltd, 64 North Row, London W1K 7LL. Tel: 020 7150 7000. Website: www. hf-uk.com

*Railway Magazine*, IPC Media Ltd, King's Reach Tower, Stamford Street, London SE1 9LS. Tel: 020 7261 5821.

*Retail Week*, EMAP Retail, 33–39 Bowling Green Lane, London EC1R 0DA. Tel: 020 7505 8000. www.retail-week. com

*Scottish Field*, Special Publications, Craigcrook Castle, Craigcrook Road, Edinburgh EH4 3PE. Tel: 0131 312 4550.

*She*, National Magazine House, 72 Broadwick Street, London W1F 9EP. Tel: 020 7439 5000. www.natmags.co.uk

*Take a Break*, H Bauer Publishing Ltd, Academic House, 24–28 Oval Road, London NW1 7DT. Tel: 020 7241 8000. www.bauer.com

*Tatler*, Vogue House, Hanover Square, London W15 1JU. Tel: 020 7499 9080. www.tatler.co.uk

*Willing's Press Guide*, Romeike Ltd, Chess House, 34 Germain Street, Chesham, Bucks HP5 1SJ. Tel: 09707 360010. E-mail: willings@romeike.com www.willingspress.com

# Useful addresses

Association of Authors' Agents, Gillon Aitken Associates Ltd, 18–21 Cavaye Place, London SW10 9PT. Tel: 020 7373 8673. E-mail: aaa:gillonaitken.co.uk www.agentsassoc.co.uk

Authors' Licensing & Collecting Society Limited (ALCS) The Writers' House, 13 Haydon Street, London EC3N 1DB. Tel: 020 7264 5700. E-mail: alcs@alcs.co.uk www.alcs.co.uk

Bibliophile Books, 5 Thomas Road, London E14 7BN. Tel: 0207 515 9222. www.bibliophilebooks.com

Booktrust, Book House, 45 East Hill, London SW18 2QZ. Tel: 020 8516 2977. E-mail: query@booktrust.org.uk www.booktrust.org.uk

Bureau of Freelance Photographers, Focus House, 497 Green Lanes, London N13 4BP. Tel: 020 8882 3315. E-mail: mail@thebfp.com www.thebfp.com

Clifford, Johnathon, 27 Mill Road, Fareham, Hampshire PO16 0TH. Tel/fax: 01329 822218. E-mail: info@vanity publishing.info www.vanitypublishing.info/index.html

Flair for Words (Cass and Janie Jackson), 14 Leonard Hackett Court, St Winifreds Road, Meyrick Park, Bournemouth BH2 6PR. E-mail: flairforwords@aol.com www.flairforwords.co.uk

How To Books Ltd, Spring Hill House, Spring Hill Lane, Begbroke, Oxford OX5 1RX. Tel: 01865 375794. E-mail: info@howtobooks.co.uk www.howtobooks.co.uk

National Association of Writers' Groups (NAWG), The Arts Centre, Biddick Lane, Washington, Tyne & Wear NE38 2AB. Tel: 01262 609228. E-mail: nawg@tesco.net www.nawg.co.uk

National Association of Writers in Education (NAWE), PO Box 1, Sheriff Hutton, York YO10 7YU. www.nawe.co.uk

National Union of Journalists, Headland House, 308 Gray's Inn Road, London WC1X 8DP. Tel: 020 7278 7916. E-mail: acorn.house@nuj.org.uk www.nuj.org.uk

Public Lending Right, Richard House, Sorbonne Close, Stockton-on-Tees TS17 6DA. Tel: 01642 604699. E-mail: authorservices@plr.uk.com www.plr.uk.com

Society for Editors & Proofreaders, Riverbank House, 1 Putney Bridge Approach, London SW6 3JD. Tel: 020 7736 3278. E-mail: administration@sfep.org.uk www.sfep.org.uk

Society of Authors, The, 84 Drayton Gardens, London SW10 9SB. Tel: 020 7373 6642. E-mail: info@societyofauthors. org www.societyofauthors.org

Society of Indexers, Woodbourn Business Centre, 10 Jessell Street, Sheffield S9 3HY. Tel: 0114 244 9561. E-mail: admin@indexers.org.uk www.indexers.org.uk

Society of Women Writers & Journalists, Wendy Hughes, Membership Secretary, 27 Braycourt Avenue, Walton-on-Thames, KT12 2AZ. Tel: 01932 702874. E-mail: wendy@ stickler.org.uk www.swwj.co.uk

Writers' Holiday in Wales at Caerleon, Anne Hobbs, School Bungalow, Church Road, Pontnewydd, Cwmbran, South Wales NP44 1AT. Tel: 01633 489438. E-mail: enquiries@ writersholiday.net www.writersholiday.net

Writers' Summer School at Swanwick, Jean Sutton, Secretary, 10 Stag Road, Lake, Sandown, Isle of Wight PO36 8PE. www.wss.org

# Index